## DEATH ON
## THE SALT FLATS OF UTAH!

The man didn't drop the Remington .41 he was gripping. Before he could do anything else with it, Longarm fired, aiming for the bastard's guts. As the man fell writhing at their feet, Longarm told the sergeant, "Take down his dying statement . . ."

**TABOR EVANS**

# LONGARM

## AND THE CARNIVAL KILLER

JOVE BOOKS, NEW YORK

LONGARM AND THE CARNIVAL KILLER

A Jove Book / published by arrangement with
the author

PRINTING HISTORY
Jove edition / July 1993

ISBN: 0-515-11136-8

Jove Books are published by The Berkley Publishing Group,
200 Madison Avenue, New York, New York 10016.
The name "JOVE" and the "J" logo
are trademarks belonging to Jove Publications, Inc.

PRINTED IN THE UNITED STATES OF AMERICA

10  9  8  7  6  5  4  3  2  1

# Chapter 1

It was a dangerously delightful dawn in the Shining Mountains. The sweet green grass of the old beaver meadow was lightly sugared with hoarfrost. The warm rays of the sun were already licking away in the dry autumn air. The aspen leaves had turned, but still shimmered against the tall dark firs further up the slopes like a swirling blizzard of gold coins. Blue breakfast smoke rose wispy above the sod roof of the low-slung log cabin out near the middle of the clearing. So a man could smell flapjacks and coffee or an early snow, depending on the wayward morning breezes in the lonely valley.

Old Lefty, the boss wrangler off the Middle Fork, watched the smoke rise a ways into the deceptively clear sky, then took the grass stem he'd been chewing from between his lips and quietly said, "It's too sneaky to show as clean-cut clouds, but you can't make out Long's Peak or even Sawtooth from here this morning. Ain't you boys glad we've less than a half day's ride back to Ward? Looks like we're getting set to be hit with a blizzard."

Deputy U.S. Marshal Custis Long of the Denver District Court had no call to argue with a rider who spent as much time up here in the high country as only a few of the more stubborn Indian nations ever had. Nobody with a lick of sense cared to haunt the Front Ranges at this altitude after, say, late September, not unless he knew for sure of a potbellied stove surrounded by at least four stout walls within no more than a few hours' ride, and not unless he had lots of faith in a storm-lashed pony's sense of direction.

The Kimoho, Shoshone, and other Ute kin who'd braved both summers and winters in the high country, before the white folks they called the Saltu Taibo took it away from them, had held it possible to live and let live with the tricky winter spirits they called the Chakwaina. Lakota and other such nations that hunted high and low on horseback held that winters in the Shining Mountains were ruled by a meaner spirit they knew as Okidi. The Cheyenne insisted the devil's name was Windigo, but agreed that a damnfool enemy who'd rather winter up this way than fight for good winter camps down on the High Plains deserved to freeze his ass.

But by now the grass was just soft and wet instead of crunchy with hoar. So Longarm, as he was better known to friend and foe alike, had a last look-see around, made sure all the others in the posse were out of sight but doubtless in position, and rose to his considerable height behind the bracken ferns he'd been slithering through to fire a polite skyward shot out of his Winchester '73 and call across a barely safe distance: "You folks in the cabin! This would be the law, federal, advising you that you're surrounded by a posse comitatus with a warrant sworn out against one Joseph Aldrich alias Kimoho Joe by the people of Boulder County, Colorado. We ain't after anybody else. So do we have us peace or war in the valley this morning?"

2

There was no answer. Longarm made the range a tad less than three hundred yards. Lefty Page must have too, for as Longarm stepped out in front of the ferns Lefty gasped, "That damn breed is said to shoot a Big .50 Sharps, and shoot it pretty tolerable, old son!"

Longarm shrugged. "They got the one door and the two windows on our side shut against the wolf winds. Meanwhile, I can hit tolerable at this range with this old saddle rifle, and a lawman who's afraid of noise is accepting his pay under false pretenses."

But he called out again, with a bit more insistence in his firm tone: "The old boys I rode out with are worried about a change in the weather and a buffalo rifle you're said to have on the premises, in that order. So how do you reckon we can assure them there's really no need to burn you all out of that old woodpile and just say it was your own fool choice?"

It seemed to be working when the dry plank door swung open and a rawboned but nicely titted-up brunette wearing no shoes and a skimpy flour-sack shift, exposing a shameful amount of shin, popped out on the puncheon porch like a worried cuckoo bird who'd just noticed it was past the hour.

She called up the slope, "Don't shoot! I swear there is nobody home but me. The mean thing left me here with only a few days' rations and barely a cord of firewood split! He heard a warrant had been swore out and lit out for Cameron Pass!"

Behind Longarm, Lefty Page sighed and said, "Shit, does he make it over the Divide before them first snows, he'll be lighting out off down the Colorado to stay with other Indian kin before we'd ever get Grand County to posse up for us."

"Let's eat this apple a bite at a time," Longarm said. He

3

raised his voice to call out to the slattern in the doorway. "I'll come on in and we'll talk about it, if you'll be kind enough to crab clear of that doorway so's I can cover it with my own muzzle, ma'am."

She sounded sincerely puzzled as she called back, "Do you think I'd be dumb enough to stand out here like a big-ass bird and lie to the law, good sir?"

To which Longarm could only reply, "That would be dumb, with me and at least a dozen others having such a clear shot at you, wouldn't it? But just you do as I say and farther along, like the old song says, we'll know more about it."

He told Lefty, "You know what to do once I make it in safe, or if I don't." Then he strode on down the grassy slope and across an ever more proddy patch of flat dooryard, softly humming that sensible old hymn as he kept the muzzle of his Winchester trained on an ever-growing and mighty spooky black patch of gaping doorway. The rawboned gal stood ominously silent, well out of anyone's line of fire, and the old Sunday-go-to-meeting words made even more sense than usual as he softly mouthed:

Cheer up, my brothers,
Walk in the sunshine,
We'll understand this all, by and by.

He did, at least a bit better, once he'd hit the porch just to one side of the door latch, ignoring the thinly clad and not bad-looking gal, and whipping inside her cabin and sliding sideways along the log wall to get his outline away from the doorway. He covered each and every stationary shape in the gloom with the muzzle of his saddle gun.

4

There was nobody there. It was easy to tell since the cabin was barely furnished and had only one spartan room.

There was no sleeping loft to study on. The one bunk bed made up at one end of the cabin was too low slung to hide anybody under it. There was no fireplace at either end. The cabin hadn't been thrown up by green-horns who'd never wintered over in the Front Range. A potbellied cast-iron stove in the dead center of the room was meant to throw more heat out sideways than up that skinny sheet-iron stovepipe. The stove was meant mostly for heating, and there was just enough flat space atop it to boil a pot or fry up a fair-sized spider of pork sausage and flapjacks. He saw she had, and had eaten most of the results within the hour, to judge by a table still cluttered with tin plates and earthenware servers and such.

The gal appeared in the doorway behind him, asking if she could come in out of the crisp morning sunshine. So he told her it was a problem to be easily solved, once she told him where the guns he couldn't seem to locate might be hiding.

She sighed and replied, "Do I look armed and danger-ous in this blamed nightgown? I begged Joe to leave me at least a squirrel gun if he expected me to get through the coming winter on my own. I begged him to take me with him. But he said a rolling stone couldn't afford no moss and . . . well, he got sort of ornery about it towards the end."

Longarm nodded soberly at her pretty but slightly misshapen heart-shaped face. "I noticed someone had hit you a pretty good lick up one side of your head, ma'am. I can see why a cuss with enough to worry about already might not want to turn his back on even an old sweetheart with a gun. Did you have the fuss

5

with him before or after you heard that that old boy he cut down in Ward had died? By the way, my friends call me Custis."

She demurely replied her name was Pansy, Pansy Yagawosier. So her high cheekbones and big sloe eyes *did* add up to some Indian blood, just like Kimoho Joe, whatever he might be to her. When she said she hadn't heard that that Saltu cowhand from down the far side of Lake Poggamoggon had died from his stab wounds, Longarm assumed Kimoho Joe might not be a man who confided his secrets to . . . whatever she was.

He asked her exactly what she was, not unkindly. She still blushed enough for it to show despite the interior gloom and her somewhat swarthy complexion. She softly replied, "We may not be married up countyways. But you got to understand we're both part Indian and, well, in the old Shining Times, when people who wished to laugh in bed together . . ."

"We'll just say you were married up with him in the eyes of that fine old creator spirit Taiowa," Longarm assured her. "Assuming he still means warm spit to you, despite that mouse he hung on you on his way out the door, I want you to pay attention and listen tight about that serious charge they want your man to answer for."

She seemed to be paying attention. So he went on. "*Heya,* when I say *they* I mean Boulder County or, even worse, the State of Colorado. Cutting cowhands at a grange dance may be rude, but it don't constitute a federal offense. I only came along because I was in Ward, winding up another matter, when they commenced to posse up. Some of the local boys recognized me from the time I had to call 'em out on a post office robbery a tad to the north of here."

6

She pouted. "We was wondering how come a famous marshal was all het up about a grange dance cutting."

He was too slick a questioner to ask who might have ridden out this way well in advance of the posse. Kimoho Joe would have been at that breakfast table if he hadn't been told by some damned someone that the white boy he'd exchanged harsh words and a few good slashes with had gone and died.

Longarm said, "Had not I owed 'em, they'd have still invited me along because I've scouted your Ho-speaking country cousins in my day and mayhaps know a few good moves, like the way they play their amusing game of *nanipka* in these mountains."

His use of a Ho term few Saltu were supposed to know inspired a burst of Kimoho that sailed over his head completely. He said so, with a sheepish grin, and added, "We both talk Saltu a heap better than I talk Ho. I learned that word for hide-and-go-seek from yet another friendly lady when I was tracking Buffalo Horn's band just the other side of South Pass. Getting back to the here and now, the partways Indian we're tracking *today* would be way better off if he was taken by someone packing a federal badge, like mine. I hardly need to tell a lady of mixed blood, no offense, what a Colorado court figures to do to a breed of ill repute who just killed a white boy."

She protested, "It was a fair fight. That cowhand cut my Joe too, you know!"

He nodded soberly. "Doubtless with a cleaner blade. I hadn't finished. If your man was to surrender to me, as a ward of the federal government, by evoking his Indian blood, I'd be proud to turn him over to the Bureau of Indian Affairs instead of your local Saltu sheriff."

She wrinkled her slightly hooked nose. "The B.I.A.

hasn't been all that generous to any of us Ho. My Kimoho granddaddy says you got to lift hair, lots of hair, like the Comanche or Sioux, before they'll treat you with any respect at all!"

Longarm sighed. "I was there when the Northern Ute got diddled out of all their lands on this side of the Divide, after they'd helped Kit Carson lick the Navajo during the bigger war back East. But your Joe would still get a fairer shake standing trial in a federal court as a noble savage. Whether his plea of self-defense held up or not, the B.I.A. ain't half as anxious to hang Indians as the State of Colorado figures to be. They only hung thirty-odd old Santee after the Big Sioux Scare of '62, and the Sioux killed way more white folks, men, women, and children, than that."

Before she could answer, Lefty Page and a couple of more regular local deputies came in to join them. Lefty said, "That center-fire dally-roping saddle he's so proud of seems to be missing from their tack shed around the back. Some of the ponies out in the paddock have had their brands run mighty artistic. We're missing a high-stepping Morgan mare he called Blue. As in blue ribbon. She's jet-black with white blaze and socks. All four hooves, of course."

One of the county lawman explained, as if Longarm needed to be told, "It's best to have all four hooves the same color, so's they wear at the same rate. I mind that pony well. Joe *did* win the blue more than once, showing her at the Lyons Stock Show last summer."

Longarm said, "Miss Pansy here told us man and beast might be trying to beat the coming winter over Cameron Pass. That's up near Sawtooth, right?"

Lefty frowned thoughtfully and declared, "I dunno. That steep north slope of old Sawtooth is covered with snow in August, and if it ain't snowing up that way right now, I just don't read the sky above these mountains as good as I used to."

The other county lawman shrugged. "Well, old Joe ain't *here*. The boys have forked the hayloft and even peered down the well. He *is* half Indian, you know. Half *mountain* Indian, and a lily-white mountain man such as Hugh Glass or old Jedediah Smith has been known to cross the Great Divide after the first snows."

Lefty grimaced. "This child ain't no maniac gone soft in the head after winter furs. Winters can be mean enough down here below the timberline. So I vote we leave Kimoho Joe to the mercy of his windy winter spirits."

He looked away from the wanted man's woman as he added with a sullen expression, "Ought to satisfy some who hold a hanging would be too good for him after all the sweating and thrashing about in his deathbed young Tommy Shaw was put through."

Pansy Yagawosier protested, "That's not fair! I was there! That white boy came over bold as brass and asked me to dance. When Joe told him I was his woman, Tommy Shaw just snickered and said he'd as soon dance with a squaw who already knew how to screw. So what would you have had Joe do?"

Longarm didn't answer. The older of the two deputies said, "He could have got you out of there peaceable, Miss Pansy. It ain't as if your kind had been invited to that grange dance, you know."

The other county lawman nodded soberly and added, not intending to sound cruel, "It's incumbent on them as horn in where they might not be welcome to keep the peace. The two of you should have knowed you might get rawhided at a dance throwed for white folk. It ain't

9

as if nobody never called you a squaw before, right?"

She looked as if she was fixing to cry, but she just stared down at the floor and murmured, "I must have been five or six the first time I asked my elders why some other kids called me that. It was not a Ho word and, even if it was, I was only about a quarter Indian. Nobody told us we weren't welcome at that grange dance. If Tommy Shaw found me so disgusting, why did he want to dance with me? Why did he want to fight over me like that?"

Longarm said, "What's done is done. The question before us now is what *we* aim to do about it. It's been my experience that when a man ain't at home he has to be somewhere else. When he puts his best saddle aboard his favorite pony, then empties the food cupboards . . . What can you tell us about such stock as he must have packing all that grub, Miss Pansy?"

She hesitated, then sighed and said, "You'll likely find out in any case. He was riding Blue and leading a paint and a buckskin when last I saw him riding into the trees up the valley. That's all I can tell you about the pack ponies he picked. Joe was the one who paid most attention to the stock out back and, well, he was acting just a mite vexed with me toward the end."

Longarm explained to the others, "He was the one as hung a mouse on her left cheekbone." Then he asked Pansy, "Exactly how much of a lead does Joe have on us, ma'am?"

She shrugged her bony shoulders. "He lit out yesterday afternoon. Late in the day. I can't tell you how he got word the Shaw kid's wounds went and mortified, just as everyone thought they was healing so fine."

The older county man demanded, "Can't tell us or *won't* tell us, Miss Pansy?"

Longarm said, "That's neither here nor nowheres. She can't be made to testify against her man in court, being the B.I.A. recognizes Indian marriage customs, whether we can or can't. Meanwhile, since it's going on eight A.M. as we're just standing here, I make it a fifteen- or sixteen-hour lead he's got on us."

He turned to Lefty Page to demand an educated guess from a man who'd ridden this range more often. Lefty said, "If he was headed for the wilder low country west of the Divide by way of old Cameron Pass, he'll have spent the first twelve hours or so getting up to a dangerous height. In more sensible weather it's the usual custom to make camp and catch some rest just below the timberline, and then push on over the Divide with plenty of light on the subject. Cameron Pass is one of the higher ones, and the hairpin trail can be a bother to a rider leading pack brutes in broad day."

One of the county lawmen said, "Kimoho Joe won't be out to cross sensible. He's more apt to be pushing his luck, and his stock, since he knows we're after him."

Longarm nodded. "Either way, I doubt we'd catch up with him alive on this side of the Divide, not so late in the game. Just for openers, we've got to ride all the way back to Ward and gather some trail supplies and extra packing stock before we light out after anyone at this time of the year."

Lefty snorted. "Speak for yourself, Longarm. I just told you suicide was not my chosen calling. If he makes it, we can scout for him some more when it's springtime. If he hasn't made it, someone will surely find his bones, way up in the sky, in the sweet by and by."

Longarm suggested, "Let's see what Boulder County and Uncle Sam between 'em want us to do. I don't see no telegraph wires this far out of town, and to tell the truth, it could commence some snowing this far down the slopes any minute now, unless that's something else I taste in this tangy morning air."

Nobody wanted to argue. They'd all tasted snow on its way before. As the others filed out ahead of him, Longarm turned back to the breed and softly said, "I won't be up this way all that much longer, Miss Pansy. I doubt my own boss, Marshal Billy Vail, would have wanted me spending even this much time on a case he won't get a lick of credit out of. But if you'd care to tell me who your man intends to winter with, over amid the headwaters of the Colorado . . ."

She said she didn't know what he was talking about. Then one of the men out front called in, "It's starting to fall! If you aim to spend your next night under a roof instead of a snowdrift, you'd best get out here and do some riding, Denver boy!"

So Longarm bade the breed gal farewell, and ducked out to find that, sure enough, small white snowflakes were drifting down from a dove-gray sky. It would have been right pretty, if they hadn't been so far from town.

Legging it back to the tree line in the wake of the others, he saw the still-green grass was already sagebrush gray under a dusting of snow. Lefty Page, striding ahead of him, was already leaving a trail a schoolmarm could have followed in worse light. But Longarm knew tracks left at the start of a snowfall wouldn't be there once the snow stopped falling. And this unseasonable dusting was sure to wreck any sign Kimoho Joe might have left along the trail. Even had there been a way to cut sign under a blanket of fresh snow, riding after anyone above the timberline right now would be asking to be frozen solid, mount and all, in the cold thin air up yonder.

Their ponies were where they had left them, in a grove of aspen, tended by a junior wrangler off the Middle Fork. As they all mounted up, Longarm cast a wistful glance back the way they'd just come. That cabin had been far warmer, and both that gal and her cooking had smelled sort of tempting.

Longarm was wearing nothing heavier than his frock coat of tobacco tweed, and once in the saddle he groped for the sheepskins he'd been smart enough to borrow in the mountain town. Pansy had explained how a white boy had gotten himself killed by misreading the signals she likely didn't know she was sending from those broody sloe eyes. A lot of blood shed by well-meaning fools on both sides seemed more the result of misread signals than a mutual suicide pact. As he finished shrugging on the sheepskins and reached for a smoke, Longarm called out to Lefty Page, riding just to his right, "Have you ever noticed how a Mex or Indian tends to avoid your eyes, as if he's feeling bashful, when he's really trying to be neighborly?"

Lefty said, "Sure. It's when a Mex smiles right *at* you, sort of sleepy, he's working his fool self up to gentle insults and a nasty fight. What about it?"

Longarm suggested, "That unfortunate Tommy Shaw might have took a pretty Kimoho breed's fluttery lashes and evasive eyes the wrong way. Our own gals tend to just look through a cuss they ain't at all interested in."

Lefty said, "The kid was an asshole to mess with *any* gal at a dance before he found out who she'd come with. I could have told a man out to change his luck where some safer Kimoho gals could be found, albeit not at that dance."

They rode on a ways through heavy snow. Then Lefty brightened and asked, "Say, didn't you know them Garson

13

gals, Miss Feather and Miss Star, last time you was up this way?"

"Not in the biblical sense," Longarm lied gallantly, as he lit a three-for-a-nickel cheroot despite the swirling snow all around. They rode on, with Lefty waxing erotic about the wild ways of those Garson gals.

It made Longarm's ears burn a mite to hear another man speculate on which of the pretty young breeds would be best in bed. For Longarm had never been able to make up his mind on that last interesting evening he'd spent in bed with the two of them.

Further up the valley, hunkered in a Hudson Bay blanket atop a granite outcrop that had been used as a lookout for generations of his mother's people, Joseph Aldrich, better known to his Kimoho kin as Honapombi, could barely make out the distant riders as they broke cover to follow the trail up the slope for a dry notch that would take them the longer but safer way back to Ward. The part-Saltu dream son of the black bear vision nodded with grudging approval as he muttered to himself, in his white father's tongue, "Old Lefty off the Middle Fork must have told 'em how the low road floods unexpectedly when the clouds hang low above the peaks to the north. By the time they get back to town the higher trails ought to be drifted as well!"

Kimoho Joe didn't do anthing but stare, even as the staring got more pointless with a serious blizzard brewing up. For no matter how deep the valley below might drift, he was only a mile and a half up north of pretty Pansy and their snug warm cabin.

He couldn't see that far now. But a man who knew his way could find his way home in total darkness, let alone in a little snow, from the short distance she'd sent him.

14

He wondered when she wanted him to come back for her. He'd known her ruse had worked as soon as he'd seen those fools heading back to Ward. It had hurt like fire to hit her pretty face like she'd told him he had to. But it seemed to have convinced them, as she'd said it might, that he'd been damn fool enough to storm off into the deadly wastes above the timberline, like a hysterical Saltu schoolmarm. It was, *hai, hau yee,* cold enough now down here among the timbered slopes!

Since discomfort for the sake of discomfort was more a Lakota than Kimoho notion, the wanted man crawfished back off his granite perch to rejoin his four ponies among the snow-dusted but windproof blue spruce he'd tethered them to. "Hear me," he announced, "we are all going over one little ridge to the lower and warmer range we know between here and the South Saint Vrain. Pansy says she doesn't think anyone will be looking for us as far away as Lyons, but she wants us to push on up to Larimer County anyway. Pansy can read."

He didn't remove his blanket as he untethered the ponies. It was snowing harder, even here among the trees. So he didn't mount up as he announced, "Hear me, we are going back to pick up my woman and the rest of our valuables. I don't want to abandon the rest of the stock and we put a lot of work into that cabin. But Pansy says it was dumb to live among Saltu who still recall our Kimoho kin. She says it will be easier to start over in Wyoming, telling Saltu we are Saltu with maybe a little Spanish blood."

He led the saddled mounts and pack ponies along a contour line until a thunderstruck pine looming gaunt and gray above them amid the swirling veils of snow told him they were in line with Pansy and that snug little cabin.

15

He led the stock down the slope, but tethered them at the tree line to ghost across the open expanse of snow-swept grass. He covered the grayness ahead of him with the muzzle of his big fifty sticking out from under his blanket.

He felt better about what he was doing as soon as he spied the penny candle Pansy had lit in that side window, as they'd agreed she would in the daytime when she was alone inside. The same candle lit anywhere else after dark, or not lit at all, was the signal they'd agreed upon to warn him off.

He still circled the cabin wide and wary, counting the ponies huddled under the overhang of the tack shed and making certain he saw none out front before he eased up to that side window for just a last quick peek inside.

He saw his Pansy fully dressed and wrapped in her own blanket as well, sitting at the table with her eyes downcast and her hands in her lap. She'd said she aimed to let the stove go out as soon as it was safe for her to begin their final packing. He didn't blame her for looking so downcast. He was going to miss this little nest in such a pretty valley. But they'd surely find another.

So the wanted man was smiling boyishly as he stepped up on the puncheon porch, stomped the snow off his boots, and opened the door to step inside, announcing, "I told you I'd likely be back before sundown, Skookumchukk!"

Then something firm as steel and cold as a banker's heart was planted firmly in the small of his back as Longarm kicked the door shut behind them and said, in as jovial a tone, "I figured you might be. First you drop that rifle. Then you shuck that blanket completely so I can watch you unbuckle your gunbelt."

Kimoho Joe dropped his big fifty, having no choice,

but said a dreadful thing to his woman as he did so.

Longarm said, "She never sold you out, old son. I'll tell you all about as we all ride on into town. But first I aim to handcuff the two of you together. Right now your woman's got my only cuffs around both her wrists. I figured that would be the best way to keep her from trying to snuff that candle again."

# Chapter 2

The undersheriff in Ward was a good sport about it when Longarm said he'd be riding on with just the one prisoner as soon as all that early snow let up. For there was many a voter around, and few were happy on either side. Indians didn't get to vote, of course, and anyway it had been a long time since there'd been enough in that neck of the woods to matter. But white folks who'd witnessed the ugly argument seemed divided on who'd been most at fault, with some holding no man had a right to low-rate another man's woman like that, while others were just as certain no damned breed had any call to cut any white man for any reason.

Nobody seemed sore at poor Pansy Yagawosier. The Shaw boy *had* gone and called her a well-broken-in squaw to her face, and Longarm could overlook a little aiding and abetting among friends. So they turned her loose to go buy some tobacco or whatever, and Longarm made certain Kimoho Joe was securely cuffed to an empty gun rack in the back of the undersheriff's substation across from the stage stop.

Lefty Page and some of the other local riders Longarm was in good with allowed they'd hang around in town in case the regular lawmen needed backing. But so far, the same unseasonable snowfall keeping Longarm and his federal prisoner in town seemed to be keeping many a friend of the late Tommy Shaw from riding in with tar and feathers, as they'd promised.

By this time Longarm was getting tired of explaining how he'd been so smart up at the Aldrich spread. So he let Lefty tell his tale to the fifth or sixth friendly gunhand who drifted in that afternoon.

As Longarm sat smoking and oiling his Winchester by the cherry-red stove near the undersheriff's desk, Lefty explained, "Longarm had wintered over with Injuns in these hills before. So he was more inclined than the rest of us to wonder why even a part-white Kimoho would want to bed down above the timberline by his fool self when he had a perfectly good woman ready and willing to tag along and warm his cold feet for him under a snowdrift."

Another rider who'd been out there broke in. "She let her man give her a shiner deliberately to sell us a whopper about him heading out alone, leaving her facing the winter undefended and almost out of grub."

Lefty nodded. "After that, we were all smart enough to wonder why any man who'd grown up in these hills would risk a run over one of the higher passes, with the air up yonder twenty below even when the wind ain't blowing."

Longarm finished reloading his dried-off and oil-wiped Winchester, but refrained from horning in. It wasn't easy as Lefty drawled on. "Having doubled back on his own trail a time or two trying to trick Shoshone and worse, Longarm just rode partways out of that valley with the rest of us, chawing on the gal's story and the parts that fit awkward. Then, knowing how tough it is to make an exact tally of distant riders in a snowstorm, he dropped out as we was passing through some aspen, circled back to dismount near the tree line, and snuck in through the blizzard till he spotted a candle going to waste by burning in broad-ass day."

From the back, Kimoho Joe protested, "It wasn't all that bright a day, and that there cabin can get gloomy when the sun ain't coming through the glass direct!"

Lefty laughed. "Tell that to some old boy who gets his candles free and don't have to pack 'em clean out to a cabin with more glass than most! I could see that had to be a signal the first time Longarm mentioned it."

Turning back to the white rider he'd been talking to, Lefty went on. "That's about the size of it. Knowing a man with a light burning in the window for him could hardly be home yet, Longarm just barged on in, handcuffed Miss Pansy at her table, and only had to wait a few minutes before old Joe walked into the trap like some self-assured pack rat!"

"It was a dirty trick," Kimoho Joe protested from his position in the rear.

Nobody seemed to pay him any mind. One of the full-time lawmen, standing by a front window, stared out it as he quietly said, "Snow seems to be letting up. Are you sure that federal court you ride for will hang that breed fair and square?"

Longarm didn't like to lie, even though he was good at it when he had to be. So he simply said, "I told you boys when I brought him in to wait here for the stage to Boulder. I mean to turn him in to the army at Camp Weld as a possible ward of the government charged with killing a white man. It'll be up to War and Interior to decide which department wants to deal with it from there. An army court-martial would be more likely to execute him.

20

But to tell you the truth, I can't see how they'd have jurisdiction. Unless they aim to declare old Joe a hostile on the warpath at a grange dance, I'd expect them to turn him over to the B.I.A. as a disciplinary problem."

"I bet they'll issue him his winter rations and tell him to just get hence and sin no more."

There came an ominous mutter of agreement from more than one man there, even though they'd all said they were on Longarm's side. So Longarm suggested, "The kith and kin of Tashunka Witko might dispute you on that point. *He* was likely expecting no more than a slap on the wrist when he gave up."

Someone asked who in blue blazes he was talking about. So Longarm set his saddle rifle aside and reached for a smoke as he replied. "Tashunka Witko translates best as Crazy Horse."

The one who'd asked just said, "Oh."

They were good old boys, and few fair-minded men doubted Crazy Horse had been done dirty, being bayoneted for reasons nobody had ever quite agreed upon, after he'd been offered honorable terms if only he'd come in and explain what he was so het up about.

The deputy by the window announced, "I never expected such an early snow to last all day, and I doubt the trails are drifted bad enough to stop that mail coach down to the county seat, or a train south from there either. They ought to be making up that mail coach even as we speak."

Another man glanced up at the Regulator Brand wall clock before declaring, "Ought to be stopping here in Ward no later than three this afternoon, if that storm's really over."

Lefty got up, strode over to that window, and had a good look at the sky outside. "Overcast is thinning," he

21

said, "and we ain't the only ones with eyes in these parts. What'll you boys bet the sun will be back out before that stage rolls in, and more important, who wants to bet me two for five a heap of Tommy Shaw's pals forecast weather and know the stage schedule good as us?"

"Powder River and let her buck!" muttered a younger hand by the front door as he hauled out his Schofield .45 to thumb a sixth round in the wheel. Younger hands were like that. More than one man there who'd already fired and been fired upon in anger looked a lot less cheered by Lefty's prophecy. A rider gone gray around the edges with a brass badge pinned to his old army shirt sighed and said, "Damn it to perdition, those are our friends and neighbors we could be talking about, and that unwashed breed back there was a known horse thief way before he started killing white folks!"

The undersheriff in charge said quietly, "You go on home to your momma if this is getting too rich for your blood, Jarvis. Just don't let me see you coming back this way with any mob if you don't want me *really* disgusted with you, hear?"

Jarvis said, "I never said nothing about not doing my damn duty. I only said I didn't *like* it all that much!"

Longarm hefted his Winchester and rose to his considerable height. "Let's not all get our bowels in an uproar, gents. I got a better idea. Like Lefty says, we know that stage will be here around three. Anyone anxious to stop me from boarding it with anyone else knows that stage will be here about three. So what if neither me nor my prisoner are anywhere in town when everyone rides in this afternoon?"

There was a moment of thoughtful silence. Then Lefty Page said, "I got more than three good ponies from the Middle Fork out back, if I follow your drift, Longarm.

You're such a tricky cuss it ain't always easy to fathom what you might do next!"

Longarm said, "Don't need three. Two will do Joe and me fine, if we get a good lead and nobody riding after us is mounted a mite better."

As he strode back to unfasten his prisoner Kimoho Joe protested, "I got to tell my woman you're dragging me clean off to Camp Weld!"

But Longarm said, "You can write her, if you know how to write and they don't mind if you do. Meanwhile, the fewer who know we're leaving right now, the better. We'll just slip out the back way, mount up, and lead our ponies tippy-toe through the woods a ways before we mount up and ride for your life."

The breed protested, "You got to let me bundle up better then. It's still freezing outside, and I got chilled to the bone just riding into town with you the way you ride."

To which Longarm could only reply with a fatherly chuckle, "Ain't it a good thing you weren't really out to haul your sissy ass up over Cameron Pass the way your woman said? Let's cut the bullshit and get your tender hide down to Camp Weld before someone tars and feathers it for you, sissy ass and all."

They wound up in Boulder half frozen to eternity but otherwise unscathed. It was after dark, but not too late to catch the last night train south, after leaving the borrowed stock and riding gear in the care of the sheriff's main office there.

Things went even smoother after that, in Longarm's opinion. By the following Monday morning the autumn weather had swung around the other way, and all that was left of that unseasonable blizzard was a patch of sooty snow here and there on the cowshit-colored lawns of Denver. There wasn't a trace of ice along Cherry Creek, despite the early hour, as Longarm ambled over the Larimer Street Bridge from his furnished digs on the less fashionable southwest side.

Not wanting to set a poor precedent, Longarm paused at a chili parlor near the federal building when he saw he was likely to get to work on time. He figured he might as well order a second coffee and some of that marble cake, seeing he was going to be chided for reporting in late in any case.

But he hadn't prepared for the sincerely worried look in the eyes of young Henry, the clerk who played the typewriter in Billy Vail's large outer office, as he drifted in less than forty-five minutes late. Henry gestured toward their mutual superior's inner office in the back as he softly warned, "I'd put out that cheroot and tiptoe in with my hat in hand if I were you, Custis."

Longarm smiled thinly and replied, "It's a good thing you ain't me, seeing it might make you so nervous, Henry. Did he say what I did, or am I supposed to just guess?"

Henry said it had something to do with that Indian, or at least part-Indian, he'd brought back with him from Boulder County. Longarm smiled innocently and ambled on back with a clear conscience, since he knew now old Billy's old lady hadn't heard that gossip up atop Capitol Hill about Longarm and that society gal visiting from back East.

The somewhat older and far shorter and stockier Marshal Vail was seated as usual behind about a quarter acre of cluttered desk. He was blowing mighty pungent cigar smoke out both nostrils and his growly mouth, to make it seem as if one of those famous London fogs had somehow wound up in his gloomy oak-paneled office. But Billy Vail's expression of pure rage seemed even worse than usual that morning.

So Longarm helped himself to the one comfortable seat on his side of the cluttered desk, and didn't ask permission to flick ashes either as he waited to see what had the ornery old cuss so . . . well, ornery.

He didn't have long to wait. Billy Vail gripped the wet end of his stubby cigar between bared teeth as he began. "I swear to a Lord without mercy, if I sent you out to fetch me just a roast beef sandwich, I'd wind up with the Jingle Bob herd being driven across my damned desk! I sent you up to Boulder County to serve a simple tax lien, and the next thing I hear you've gone riding out after a wild Indian wanted locally. Let me repeat, *locally*, you silly son of a—"

"Watch it, Billy Vail!" Longarm cut in. "*I* work for you. My folks don't. As to how I carried out the chores I was sent on, I *served* that demand for back taxes, to the next of kin. The old boy who failed to make good on his improved homestead claim meant Uncle Sam no disrespect. He died from a mortified appendix, like old Brigham Young did, and just never got the chance to inform the Bureau of Land Management by mail."

Vail growled, "Never mind dead nesters. That was all in the wire you sent days ago. What in thunder ever possessed you to horn in on a penny-ante dance cutting?"

Longarm said, "Some of the boys up to Ward rode with me the time we had that serious post office robbery up that way. To tell the truth, I never expected the case to get so complicated. But seeing Joe Aldrich was at least part Indian, and seeing he was likely to get as informal a trial from a Colorado jury as Cockeyed Jack McCall

25

got as a backshooter who'd backshot somebody far more popular . . ."

"Damn it," Vail said, "McCall *did* shoot James Butler Hickok in the back!"

"In the Number Ten Saloon in Deadwood, Dakota Territory," Longarm insisted. "Meaning the purely local Colorado court that not only condemned McCall to death but hung him didn't have a lick of jurisdiction over either Wild Bill or the other drunk who killed him. McCall was doubtless guilty, and I wasn't there in any case. I *was* there in Ward when mention was made of a hanging being too good for a Kimoho cocksucker. On top of which, the breed might have a plea of self-defense a fair lawyer could defend him with in a halfways fair court. So I decided it might be best to bring him in as a half-ass Indian and see what kind of a shake the army or B.I.A. might be willing to give him."

Vail rummaged atop his desk as he grumbled, "I know why you done what you done, you asshole, and don't say your ass don't belong to *me*! Meanwhile the War Department says it has no policy papers on any Kimoho nation. So they've turned the matter over to the B.I.A., and guess what. The B.I.A. has the Kimoho listed as an *extinct* branch of the North Ute nation."

Longarm chuckled. "I met two sisters called Feather and Star who seemed sort of lively for extinct gals too. I'm glad we've cleared up the mystery as to just who those folk called Kimoho must have been, back when they were more numerous. Both them sisters say it means something like Friendly People. I never had call to doubt either one of 'em."

Vail snapped, "Never mind any friendly Kimoho gals. Thanks to you we seem to be stuck with a less friendly one. If his defense evokes his Indian blood, and they'll get him hung for certain if they don't, the B.I.A. will want him tried in an agency court as some damned sort of North Ute."

Longarm sincerely stared about for a cuspidor or ash-tray before, finding neither on his side of the desk, he flicked the ash he just had to flick on the mock-Persian rug. Then he demanded, "What do *we* care? It's out of our hands now, right?"

To which Vail replied murderously, "Wrong. In case you were in bed with that widow who ought to know better up on Sherman through an entire Indian war, you know by now that the North Ute lost, and got their surly selves marched clean over to Utah Territory."

Longarm nodded soberly. "I do. It was you who sent me to arrest that early crooked agent they had, left over from Grant's Indian Ring. I've seen worse reservations than they wound up on over yonder."

He took another drag on his cheroot. "Does any of this conversation have a thing to do with Kimoho Joe Aldrich?"

Vail said, "It does. The B.I.A. has requested that we, as the stupid-ass arresting authority, transport the pris-oner from that stockade at Camp Weld, where he don't belong, to the Indian Police post at the Uinta North Ute Agency, Utah Territory, where he does!"

Longarm gaped and gasped, "At this time of the year? You can't get within a hundred miles of that remote mountain agency by rail at any time, and once winter sets in seriously, you can't hardly get in or out at all!"

Vail said, "I told them as much. That's doubtless why they want one of us, instead of one of them, to transport the rascal."

"Damn it, I could wind up snowed in with all them Utes for Lord knows how long!" Longarm said.

To which Vail sweetly replied, "That's why I'm sending you instead of a deputy with sense enough to stay out of petty local disputes. It was your grand notion to make a federal case out of the grange dance cutting. So now the case is all yours. Henry ought to have your travel orders all typed up by the time your train leaves this afternoon. So you'd best get your ass out to Camp Weld and pick up the old boy you'll be spending some time with betwixt here and out yonder where the bloodthirsty breed belongs!"

# Chapter 3

As a man who'd studied on the Game of Life, Longarm had come to the wry conclusion that since none of us figured to beat the house in the end, we could either get up from the only table there was and jump off a cliff, or just play the damn cards we were dealt for just as long as old Lady Luck kept dealing. For our chips would be gone soon enough, and meanwhile, sometimes you got a hand that made the game seem less pointless, or at least more fun.

The tedious train ride out to Utah Territory commenced as a piss-poor hand. There was a right handsome brunette on board, traveling alone and seemingly bored as hell with her own company. But Longarm was saddled with the boring company of an ever more sullen breed he couldn't risk leaving unguarded in their private compartment, even in cuffs and leg irons.

Kimoho Joe was wearing neither, of course, as they rode through the ever increasing gloom of a dying autumn day. Longarm respected the U.S. Constitution too much to inflict the cruel and unusual punishment of manacled limbs on anyone he had the drop on. So he only cuffed the breed to a Pullman seat now and again when he stepped out in the corridor to order them both some refreshments. That lonesome brunette sure seemed to prowl the corridors a lot.

But he never started up with her, even though his prisoner was such dull company. The sullen shit forgot to say thanks when a man offered him a smoke or ordered him a dessert with his supper from the dining car—and that mince pie with whipped cream had been *good*!

Longarm couldn't even get him to laugh at the joke about the old boy from back East and the medicine man's daughter. So he figured it had to be the Indian blood. Such blood flowed stronger in some breeds, and few Indians had ever cottoned to the notion of not wandering free as big-ass birds.

The early planters far to the southeast had had to send all the way to Africa or Ireland for bond servants because the Indians living all around them just commenced to mope and stop living as soon as you managed to convince them they were your slaves. Half the tales of the army murdering Indian prisoners were really inspired by captive Quill Indians simply going loco while locked up, and beating themselves to death with the walls and bars of their cells, the way a wild bird could flutter itself to death in a cage.

So telling Kimoho Joe there was a fifty-fifty chance that the B.I.A. would buy his plea of self-defense only seemed to make him feel more sorry for his fool self. It was true he'd likely have to stay in the North Ute Police Stockade while awaiting at least a hearing. Longarm said he didn't know how long that might be. He didn't want to have a freshly cleaned suit all spattered with the blood and brains of a fluttering big-ass bird.

They got into Ogden, near the Great Salt Lake, in the wee small hours Henry should have figured on, dad

30

blast his typed-up travel orders, so Longarm marched his prisoner to the city jail near the depot.

As he'd hoped, the Gentile desk sergeant recalled Longarm as a pal of his Mormon Police Commissioner, and said they'd be proud to put a federal prisoner up for the night.

When Longarm explained who Kimoho Joe was and what he'd been charged with, Lady Luck relented about the tedious cards she'd been dealing of late, and had the desk sergeant say, "In that case we'll just put him in with another red rascal we picked up, drunk and on the warpath in a house of ill repute. They can swap mean lies about us in Ute till we figure out what to do with 'em."

As a turnkey led Kimoho Joe, sobbing and cussing, away, Longarm gave the desk sergeant the name of the hotel he'd be staying for a few hours, adding, "I didn't know this railroad town—no offense—had jurisdiction over Utes. Are they supposed to stray so far north of their Uinta agency?"

The Utah lawman answered, "Not drunk and disorderly. Ain't certain they're allowed this far from home cold sober. But that's for their own agent to say, once he gets 'em back. Couple of Indian Police will be here for the rascal anytime now. We wired 'em we were holding him a good three days ago, and man, that's one sad as well a sober Indian back there. The company of your prisoner ought to cheer him up. *How* long did you say we could keep him for you?"

Longarm grinned thoughtfully and decided, "Mayhaps longer than I'd originally planned. I was aiming to head south with him after a few hours' rest for the both of us. It's a son-of-a-bitching ride over many a windy rise, after you leave the narrow-gauge."

He hauled out two cheroots and presented one to the desk sergeant as he added, "I doubt even Billy Vail, the one and original devotee to chickenshit chores, would begrudge me a few days' layover up here in Ogden in order to save as much as two weeks on the trail, Lord willing and the weather holds back."

He thumbed a match aflame for the both of them, but found the Utah lawman was ahead of him. The desk sergeant took a drag on the free smoke and opined, "Well, them Indian Police would be able to transport your prisoner down to their agency good as you, seeing they already know the way and won't be heading nowheres else. You say you'll be at the Union Hotel, in case the day-watch commander cares?"

Longarm said that was about the size of it, and they parted right friendly. He'd checked the modest extras he'd brought along with the railroad baggage smashers at the depot. He'd meant to hire such riding gear as they might need at the end of that second narrow-gauge leg of their tedious route. He felt no call to check the shit out at this ungodly hour. The hotel would supply all the soap, towels, and such he'd need on this side of a comfortable stretch-out with no damned old sullen prisoner to keep an eye on.

He saw the coffee shop was still open, if it ever closed, as he crossed the paved but silent avenue between the depot and the hotel. He recalled the hotel as all right from earlier trips out this way. He did have a little rumbling in his gut, now that he studied back on how long it had been since he'd eaten. But first things came first and so he ambled on in, woke up the old fart nodding at the phony mahogany desk, and booked himself a corner room with a bath—or at least a running-water sink a man could piss in if he had to.

32

When the room clerk asked how long he meant to stay, Longarm told him truthfully he didn't know. The older man said a silver dollar would cover him till noon. So Longarm snapped two on the desk beside the sign-in ledger, and allowed he'd kill any son of a bitch who woke him up that early.

Then, lest early morning hunger pangs disturb the rest he'd just paid good money for, he strode through the lobby entrance to that coffee shop in hopes of something more tempting than that last stale sandwich aboard the train.

That handsome brunette he'd noticed traveling west with him was seated at a table near the counter. Her figure was even better than he'd suspected, now that she'd shed her tan travel duster to perch there, looking sort of proddy in a summerweight dress of pink and white calico and a white straw boater.

She was not alone. Two young gents dressed rougher sat at table with her while a third, with the brim of his grimy Stetson laced with that fuzzy rabbit-skin string the Paiute twist by the mile and sell cheap, had hauled up an extra chair to sort of lean over her shoulder and talk right in her ear.

She didn't seem to be enjoying what he was saying, but Longarm had noticed on the train what a flirty gal she seemed to be, and it was no federal offense to take an unescorted woman up on such sassy eyes. So he just mosied over to the counter and asked the far fatter gal behind it when those glazed donuts had been baked.

She assured him they were fresh. So he bought half a dozen with enough coffee to dunk them in. He usually took his coffee neat, but he asked her to put plenty of canned milk in it, lest it sucker him out of all that sleep he'd just paid for.

As he turned with his tray, looking for a place to set it down, the brunette waved at him and said, "Over here, for heaven's sake! I *thought* that was you. But I wasn't sure until you moved over there under the light! What on earth are *you,* of all people, doing here in the wilds of Utah Territory?"

The cowhand purring in her ear protested, "Aw, we ain't all that wild, Miss Joy."

Longarm was sorely tempted to let herself get out of it as best she could. But the poor little thing looked so trapped as she smiled with her mouth and begged him with her eyes that he somehow found his fool self moving their way with his damned donuts. But as he started to put his tray down, clean over on the far side of her table, the possessive-looking one in the show-off hat scowled up at him to declare flat out, "There's no more seats at Miss Joy's table, and even if there was, nobody's invited you to join us, pilgrim."

Longarm set the tray down, reached for a bentwood chair facing another table, and whipped it around to sit down on it astride so his boots were planted for a sudden rise. He politely but firmly replied, "This chair will do me, and it seems to me I did hear a lady inviting me over, old pard."

Then he nodded to the gal he'd never seen before to say, "I can't say I expected to meet you out this way, Miss Joy. I just got off a night train, with no errands that can't wait until business hours, the other side of sunrise. You staying here at the Union too?"

The one with the fuzzy hat brim growled, "She is, with *us,* so why don't you go on about your own damned business before somebody gets hurt?"

This hardly seemed the time to have his gun hand filled with soggy donut. So Longarm dunked left-handed as he quietly replied, "I wasn't planning on hurting nobody. You just let me know when you're ready to go on upstairs, Miss Joy, and I'll be proud to see you safely to your door."

"I'm counting to ten," the wilder of the three announced, and actually started counting, although slow enough for Longarm to ask the one closer to him on the left, "Is this to be a private funeral or will it be attended by the general public?"

The younger hand shrugged and murmured, "I only fight when it's worth my while, and ain't you that gambling man they call Big Casino over Leadville way?"

Longarm didn't answer, the one doing the counting having reached an ominous seven. The one he'd just been talking to slid his own chair back, well back, and nodded at the kid across from him to say, "I reckon they both mean it. You too, ma'am. We'd best *all* ease out of their line of fire."

The girl called Joy stared in dawning horror as the full meaning of the cowhand's laconic words sank in. The one seated closer to her rose to move further back, murmuring, "There's no stopping old Lockport once he's like that, and the Colorado hat and big mustache on this other gent adds up to someone just as stubborn."

Longarm had no idea who any of these total strangers thought he might be. He was feeling more like the king of fools than any grown man as he casually let one hand drop out of sight when the one they called Lockport got to nine. It would have been more slippery than smart for either to draw and fire on the count of nine. For all this shit was taking place in the middle of a good-sized town with a heap of grown men rolling out of bed about then to get dressed and, if need be, strap on some guns of their own.

Winning a gunfight was only a part of it. Excusing yourself for having started one could be the real bitch, and so there was a good chance the lovesick asshole was bluffing.

He got to ten, and must have hoped Longarm was bluffing when he said, "Your time is up. This is your last chance to crawfish out of here alive. I mean it."

Longarm nodded soberly and said, "I'm sure you do. Are you ready to leave yet, Miss Joy?"

She sprang to her feet and snatched up her duster as all four men rose, slower but paying more attention to their balance. The two who'd just been watching moved further back. The one who'd just accused Longarm of being someone else pleaded, "Let it go, Lockport! If he's who I think he is he's bad medicine!"

Lockport growled, "I reckon *I* can be bad medicine too. Do you aim to stand your ground and die or light out and live, you son of a . . ."

Then he was staring into the unwinking muzzle of a .44-40 a suddenly serious-looking Longarm had seemingly created out of thin air. So he froze, his own hands still polite, while Longarm smiled wolfishly and softly suggested, "Let's leave our folks out of this. Miss Joy, I'd like you to just saunter on into the lobby now, and I'll be along when I'm finished here."

She started to say something. He snapped, "*Move* it, girl!" So she did. Not even the thunderstruck fat gal on the far side of the counter bothered to follow her out with their eyes. But Longarm had a good sense of timing. So as soon as he figured she was gone, he nodded at the cuss he was covering and asked, pleasantly enough, if they were finished there.

Lockport grumbled, "You got the drop on us. Don't ask me how. So I reckon she's your'n, for now. But I ain't forgetting this, Big Casino!"

Longarm sighed. "I wish you would. To begin with, that ain't my name. As to Miss Joy, she ain't with either one of us. Had you been able to grasp that we might not have wound up scaring one another like this for no sensible reason."

"I was doing fine till *you* come along," Lockport insisted.

Longarm said, "No, you wasn't. You don't know much about gunplay neither. So allow me to leave you with a bit of fatherly advice. I have read Ned Buntline's *Wild West Magazine* too. I enjoy a comedy as well as the next cuss. But I don't take that Code of the West he writes about too serious. Had I wanted an easy notch in my gun grips I'd have blown you away at the count of, say, five or six after you'd been kind enough to warn me in advance you were looking for a fight."

He aimed a bit lower for emphasis as he added sternly, "Lucky for you I ain't dumb enough to notch my gun grips or take fool kids showing off for the gals that serious. So now I mean to back out of here friendly, and don't none of you follow unless you really mean it this time. Like the big chief said, I have spoken."

Nobody made a move as he calmly backed out of the coffee shop, gun in hand to cover everyone there but the counter gal. As he made it to the lobby archway one of them marveled, "That was cutting her too close for *this* child, Lockport! Next time you go up against the real thing you just leave me the hell out of it, hear?"

"Aw, he wasn't all that tough," Lockport grumbled, adding, "Nobody got shot, right?"

Longarm didn't linger to listen to such hot air. Backing past a startled bellboy, he put his sidearm away under his frock coat and swung to head up the carpeted stairs two at a time. He'd naturally pocketed his room key before heading into all that nonsense in the coffee shop. He found the brunette in an alcove on the second landing up, crying fit to bust into the kerchief she was sort of gnawing on.

He paused there—it was only polite—to assure her, "It's over, with less noise than you seem to have anticipated, Miss Joy. Why don't we just get you to your room and say no more about it now."

She said, "I'm afraid to go to that room, down on the second floor. That's what I'm doing this far up the stairs. You see, I told those dreadful boys who I was and let them know I was staying here at the Union before I knew . . . what sort of boys they were."

He started to say something dumb. But it would have been a tad optimistic to suggest a determined lothario with a gun couldn't get a room number out of an old clerk if he really wanted to. So he said, "Let's study on how you got that old boy so determined about you, Miss Joy. I was just telling him how foolish it can be to start things you don't really mean to finish, and—no offense—you acted a mite sassy with me earlier on that night train."

She stared wide-eyed up at him through her tears, protesting in a very convincing tone, "I don't know what you're talking about! I never acted any way with you on any train. I never saw you before in my life until I grasped at a straw in that coffee shop just now!"

He frowned back at her uncertainly, muttering, "Pretending I was some gent you knew would have worked as good, or bad, whether you'd had me in particular in mind or not. But don't you remember all the traipsing back and forth you were doing aboard that night train?"

38

She nodded innocently and explained, "Every time I got comfortable there was this silly old Mormon with a white beard and eight wives, he said. I don't know whether he was out to convert me or make me his ninth wife, but he seemed intent on following me all up and down that train. You say you noticed?"

Longarm cocked a brow. "Not him. You. I'd hate to call a pretty lady a liar but unless I'm going blind . . . Hold on, might you ever have call to wear glasses, mayhaps just for reading, Miss Joy?"

She lowered her long wet lashes with a sigh, confessing, "Well, I fear I may be just a shade myopic."

So he laughed more surely. "There you go. I was just talking about gals' eyes the other day and, well, white gals with . . . more usual vision let us brutes know they ain't interested by sort of looking through us. On the other hand, a gal staring keen at a cuss, or a near-sighted gal who might not know *what* in thunder she could be staring at, might inspire anyone from a Mormon elder to a dumb old me to mistake her true intent."

She answered hesitantly, "Well, that silly Lockport did seem to think I'd invited him and his pals over to my table for some reason. I fear I didn't understand their full meaning before I'd tried to fend them off with, well, a big-sister approach to their approach."

Longarm started to lead her back down to her own floor. Then he said, "I ain't sure I'd feel comfortable behind my own door, not knowing who could be pounding on *your* door, and come to study on it, that bullyboy did promise to come after *me* some more. So let's commence with how much baggage you got and where, Miss Joy."

She said, "I've only an overnight bag in my room down below. I left my Saratoga trunk and bigger bags at the depot across the way. You see, had we gotten in at a more reasonable hour . . ."

"Great minds run along the same channels, ma'am," he said. With a more certain grip on her elbow he gently swung her around to head down, explaining, "I've stayed at the Pacific, down the block, and it's just as clean and no dearer. So why don't we snatch your one bag on the fly and sneak you out the back of this hotel to a room nobody knows about in another."

She hesitated, then hugged closer to him, allowing that that was the most sensible suggestion any man had made to her since she'd left Cheyenne. So that was what they did.

It was easy. They encountered nobody, friend or foe, once they picked up her modest baggage and, at his suggestion, left both their room keys on her unmade bed for the hotel help to find.

On the way to the Pacific he explained who he was, and assured her he could charge the extra nights, or in this case early mornings, to his traveling expenses. It actually had to come out of the six to twelve cents a mile and seventy-five cents per diem he'd put in for once he got back to Denver. But he felt no call to brag about the few cents he was losing on the deal. He just paid the damned Pacific for adjoining rooms, and hauled her and her damned overnight bag up to the damned fourth floor, where at least the early morning rumble, and aroma of horse, might not disturb either one of them as they lay slugabed after sunrise.

He was about ready to get right in bed. But the brunette seemed on edge and wistful every time he mentioned leaving her alone in her own hired room. So he asked her permission to smoke, and sat on the bedstead beside her as the sky outside got ever lighter and some old redwing commenced to spin its song at them from a cottonwood across the alley her windows were facing.

She said she was an advance gal for a traveling tent show, paid to hit a town first and arrange for the advertising, lot, permits, graft, and so forth. When he asked if she'd ever worked for the more famous Sells Brothers show that toured mostly west of the Big Muddy, she confessed she hadn't, but that she'd always wanted to. She said she had old chums touring with Sells Brothers, and asked him if he'd ever heard of Miss Irene, the Incredible India Rubber Girl.

He had indeed, but only admitted he'd taken in the big show the last time it had passed through Denver. He'd promised the Incredible he'd respect her in the morning, and it was nobody's beeswax whether such a pretty little thing could screw a man and lick his balls at the same time.

But even the mention of good old Irene, wherever she might be all contorted at the moment, made Longarm decide it was time he got himself out of there before he proved himself as forward as old Lockport.

This other gal had already come close to getting somebody killed in defense of her myopic morality. So he got to his feet, trying not to yawn in her pretty face as he announced, "I'll sure want a look at your own tent show if I'm still in town when it gets in, Miss Joy. Meanwhile, if I don't totter next door whilst the tottering's good, I'm likely to fall sound asleep on you right here."

She rose to face him, close, as she murmured, "I wouldn't mind if you fell asleep with me afterwards."

So there it was, right out in the open as the sky blushed rosy outside. She looked so swell he just had to haul her in and kiss her good, lest she take him for a sissy who couldn't take a hint.

41

She kissed back French-style and sobbed, "Oh, yes, yes, stop teasing me this way!" He lowered her back down to the mattress and hoisted up her calico skirts to see if she really meant it.

She did, he figured, as soon as he noticed she wore nothing under her skirts above the lace garters holding up her black silk stockings. Even more interesting, she'd shaved her crotch bare as a baby's behind. So he commenced to strum her pink banjo for her as they lay side by side across the counterpane, swapping spit as she fumbled with his buttons. Then she had his old organ-grinder out stiff, and marveled, "Oh, good heavens, it's even bigger than she said and . . . would you mind if we started with me on top, Custis?"

He said it might make even more sense if she gave him a chance to get out of his gun rig at least. So she laughed like the mean little kid she was turning out to be, and helped him strip completely as the sun came all the way up outside.

She said the broad day made her bashful as she forked a silk-sheathed thigh across his naked hips to lower herself onto him in her calico dress, although with the skirts hiked up about her trim waist so he could spy her bare ass in the pier glass across the room by the closet door.

He found the sight of his shaft sliding up in her exciting, while she seemed to find the feel of it downright frightening! She bit her lower lip and settled down, wide-eyed, until she had to stop with a good inch of him still left out in the cold and gasp, "Good heavens, it's touching bottom and I could swear there was more of it to come!"

He moaned, "There sure is, and you're so tight I fear I'm going to come way ahead of you!"

But in the end, he only came a few strokes ahead of her, because she suddenly stopped acting coy and proceeded to slither up and down the full length of his erection, faster and faster as they both felt him hitting bottom with every stroke, until he shot his wad and she clamped down, hard, moaning, "I felt that, and it was just lovely, but now let's really *do* it!"

So they did, with her finishing her own orgasm in that same sort of prim position, then peeling her dress off over her head to unpin her long black hair and really show off as he lay on his back, with her high heels dug far apart into the bedding on either side of him so she could really gyrate her bare shaven pelvis with her palms planted on his hairy chest.

It got him so hot he just had to roll her on her own back so he could do some gyrating of his own with her high-buttons locked around the nape of his neck, and no more bullshit about it being in too deep as he pounded her to glory with the morning sun smiling in at them and that redwing cheering them on fit to bust.

It was after they'd paused for their second wind, sharing one of his pungent cheroots, when he got her to sheepishly admit she *had* been trying to pick him up aboard that night train.

She said, "It was your own fault, you bashful thing. That other girl you teased half to death when Sells Brothers were in Denver told me all about you. So when I spied you aboard the train, I had to find out whether half the things Irene said about you could be true."

He let some smoke go and muttered, "I noticed Irene had a healthy interest in . . . nature. But I'd rather hear about those other nature lovers you damn near got me into a fight with this morning. Is it safe to say I *did* beat a fellow man out of some mighty fine slap-and-tickle?"

She began to toy with his well-sated shaft as she demurely told him, "I just said I'd seen *you* first aboard that night train. Even if I hadn't, there are limits to a girl's sense of adventure and, well, when that silly cowboy said all three of them were going to do me at the same time, I confess I was sorry I'd allowed even one of them to sit down beside me."

Longarm took a deep drag and didn't answer. What was done was done, and he supposed it could be taken as sort of flattering. Not sure how to take his silence, Joy insisted, "All three of them could have used a shave for certain, and probably a bath as well. I'd be fibbing if I said I'd never considered what it might be like with *two* men at the same time. But the only way it would work with three sounds sort of disgusting, if not downright dangerous."

He passed her the cheroot, saying, "Spare me the picture. Didn't your mother ever tell you us brutes prefer a gal who's never even considered kissing another man? It helps if she's learned to blow the French horn and studied Greek on her own as well. We admire such skills, but just don't want to hear about hairy-chested teachers."

She took a drag on his smoke and said innocently, "The older man who first got me to shave down there said much the same thing. You men are so impractical about your favorite pastime. We girls are ever so much more interested in doing things right. I think it was Catherine the Great who used to have her ladies-in-waiting test handsome guardsmen she'd chosen. I've no doubt Her Majesty saved herself many a dreary night with a poorly endowed pretty boy by having another woman screw him first."

Longarm grimaced and replied, "They say that's why the present Prince of Wales prefers women married to

44

his friends. Saves the fat slob from finding out the hard way whether they're any good in bed or not. But I dunno, call the rest of us romantic, but finding out for ourselves beats going sloppy seconds, even with a pal going first."

She handed back the cheroot, and got on her hands and knees to declare, "Well, since you refuse to invite a pal in to help a poor girl out, I guess I'll just have to get that silly thing hard for us the way someone you don't want to hear about might have taught me."

Whether she'd been funning or not, the crack about another man kept him soft longer than usual, despite her skilled sucking. But once she did have it up for him again, he was willing to forgive that other son of a bitch. For he sure had broken her in mighty fine.

# Chapter 4

By the time she'd had enough, the town outside was
wide awake and folks were bustling about the hotel
corridors. Joy said she had to make it to the bank before
it closed that afternoon, and suggested they get some
sleep. He asked whether she'd be in the market for
an armed escort going or coming. When she explained
she only meant to present a letter of credit and make
sure the local branch of a cross-country bank honored
the checks her traveling show would be paying their
local bills with, Longarm allowed they'd best sleep dis-
creetly in the separate rooms they'd checked into. They
could get together later that evening if she meant what
she'd said about wanting to try a few things she'd only
read about.

She said he was being an old fuss about the hotel
chambermaids. He said he wasn't ashamed of her company, and might not have cared who knew how fond they
were of one another had not he been riding for a reform
Administration in a territory run by a church.

As he dressed he elaborated. "The Salt Lake Temple
ain't all too pleased to have all us Gentiles, or outsiders,
swilling coffee and spitting tobacco up this way. But

once you allow a railroad town, you got to put up with heaps of railroad workers and worse. But if we tend to think they're a mite odd, they're inclined to gasp aghast at the way *we* carry on, whether we're carrying on or not. So I can't afford to have any tales about my private affairs getting back to my boss in Denver by way of the Salt Lake Temple. I'm one of the few Gentile federal agents the somewhat fussy Saints seem to trust, and I'd like to keep it that way."

She archly suggested he really meant to seduce some Mormon gal out in the hall as she slept off the effects of his ever so discreet long-donging. He laughed, pinched both naked nipples as he kissed her *adios* for now, and never even saw another gal as he slipped out and undressed some more right next door.

Since he'd meant to retire much earlier, he dropped off as soon as his head hit the pillow, and must have slept a good six hours alone before something rapping on his room door woke him up.

It was Joy. She came in neatly groomed in a fresh summer dress of cornflower blue to ask if he'd been meaning to sleep all day. She'd already been to the bank and taken care of a dozen other errands. She said she'd had all her baggage delivered next door, and asked if he wanted her to strip down again in this room or the other one.

He chuckled fondly and replied, "Both. But hold the thought for now, little darling. I got some chores of my own to tend to, and it was good of you to wake me when you did."

She offered to get on top with her dress on again. But he'd already washed his love-sweated hide at the corner stand before flopping in bed. So he protested that he'd rather start out with no distractions in mind after he'd

47

made sure nobody else would be pestering them. She relented when he said he'd buy her a warm meal to restore her full strength before they got in bed again.

He knew he needed a shave by then, but felt he was presentable enough to go to jail, even as a visitor. So that was where he went first.

The desk sergeant said the day-watch commander wanted a word with him in the back. Having been warned the cuss was a Saint, Longarm resisted the temptation to offer a cheroot, or light one for himself, as the somewhat older Utah lawman, dressed more like an undertaker, shook hands and offered him a seat in an office a mite more cheerful than Billy Vail's.

This was the first time Longarm had met this particular Ogden man. But the Saint, who answered to Captain Dexter, said he'd heard good things about Longarm. "You were traveling with that other touring show a spell back, as I recall. Did you ever catch those Hebrew haters who were out to kill the French actress running that outfit?"

Longarm nodded. "In Virginia City, with the help of a gunfighter nobody knew to be Jewish. Last I heard, the Divine Miss Sarah Bernhardt was planning another retirement tour of the States, seeing as she made out so grand the last two times she retired."

Dexter nodded and declared, "She put on a fine show here, I understand. But to tell the truth, I can't say I've heard as many kind words about that Palmer and Lewis tent show you seem to have under your wing this time."

Longarm smiled incredulously, but didn't ask how Dexter knew he had any connection with Joy or her outfit. Ogden was a fair-sized town when you counted all the railroaders and transients. But once you narrowed the gossip-gathering to the hard core of Saints who ran it . . . well, he'd warned old Joy not to holler like that when she was coming on top. So he could only smile sheepishly at the older man and explain, "I ain't riding herd on any tent show, sir. As they must have told you out front, I deposited a federal prisoner with them last night, or leastways, early this morning. I've yet to let my boss know by wire whether I have to go on with the cuss or not."

Dexter nodded. "I doubt it. Those Indian Police wired us earlier today that they'd made it to American Fork and hoped to transfer to a northbound due here sometime this evening."

He looked away awkwardly, and added, "I was hoping you might be able to shed more light on that tent show. You know, we don't try to impose our own notions on outsiders, and it's a simple fact that we have more Gentiles than Saints in this part of the territory on any Saturday night it's not snowing. But we've heard odd things about that particular tent show and, well, I wish I had someone way more worldly about cigarettes, whiskey, and games of chance to advise me on the matter."

Longarm shrugged. "I know you Saints don't approve of the cigarettes and whiskey. It ain't for me to say whether you want to allow either out at the fairgrounds. As to games of chance, I have yet to visit a tent show midway offering the suckers anything like a chance. The suckers know the games are rigged and don't care all that much, unless they're suckers indeed. The fun is in *trying* to win. The stakes are small, the prizes are cheap trash, so it ain't all that important. Another tent show gal I used to know was convinced there'd be more trouble if more suckers won. It's hard to feel jealous when nobody can really knock all the iron milk bottles over. She said they

49

worked that with a springy wire or two, to keep one or two bottles standing after some teasing teetering. Then there's that wheel of fortune with the secret brake, and there's the games like blackjack where the dealer don't *have* to cheat, unless he's in a hurry, because the odds against a sucker are right there for anyone but a sucker to see."

Captain Dexter said, "The Lord protects fools at least as much as they-who-have-eyes-but-will-not-see deserve. We've issued permits to such outfits as Sells Brothers in the past with no great harm done to any of our very own. But a circus with a sideshow is one thing. A sideshow alone, or collection of hoop throws and freak tents, is another! We've heard Palmer and Lewis allows more games of chance, or at least games, than most, for higher stakes. And just this morning we got a tip from a waitress at the Union Hotel coffee shop that a notorious gambling man called Big Casino has come to town."

"That was *me*!" Longarm said with an astonished grin, explaining, "Some uncouth country boys pestering a lady in that coffee shop took me for somebody notorious when I made 'em leave her be. One of 'em called me Big Casino. Big casino is a game, like draw poker or old maid. I'm sure glad they didn't call me Old Maid. There must be dozens of tinhorns called Big Casino, Two-Bit Ante, or even Old Maid, just like there's dozens of riders called Slim, Tex, or Kid. I don't recall any serious wanted flyers on any particular Big Casino, and in any case, I seem to be the only one here."

Captain Dexter looked relieved and declared, "Sometimes I get the feeling that a jar of olives busted on the walk gets reported to the police as a wagon load of watermelons over a cliff. The city council's already issued a permit to that brunette you don't know all that well. So it's out of my hands in any case, and I was more concerned with those rumors of serious gambling and sinister drifters such activities attract."

Then he made a liar of himself by swinging back to stare sort of puppy-dog-wistful at Longarm, asking, "I don't suppose, after those Indian Police light out with that prisoner we took off your hands, you'd care to look that tent show over for us, seeing you'd know better than your average Saint just how right or wrong they might be running things?"

Longarm had no call to hedge as he answered simply, "If I got the time, I will. If I ain't, I won't. It all depends on how soon I'll be free to head back to Denver and how soon they'll have the midway set up. I enjoy a tent show as well as the next man. But I have a boss to answer to, and old Billy can be a real spoilsport if there ain't no federal angle to a complaint."

Captain Dexter said that sounded better than an outright refusal. So they shook on it and parted friendly, with Longarm lighting up the moment it was polite to do so, out on the sunny walk.

He was puffing contentedly a block away when a uniformed copper badge fell in step beside him. The lawman, who was likely Mormon, didn't tell him to put out that infernal cheroot. He said, "The sarge sent me after you. We just figured out you're the one who Miss Tillie, the counter gal at the Union Coffee Shop, says Lockport Krankheit and the Miller boys are gunning for."

Longarm sighed and said, "I just explained my little run-in with old Lockport and his pals to Captain Dexter. If your Miss Tillie is a pleasantly plump twenty-five or so with chestnut hair and big old eyes to match, I noticed she seemed to be taking things way more serious than me."

The local lawman replied, "That's likely because she knows the boys you were rawhiding better than you, Deputy Long. Lockport is a killer. The worst kind of killer. His rich widowed momma has a whole law firm at her beck and call, and those Miller boys tag along to swear under oath that the other feller drew first!"

Longarm grimaced. "This morning I *did*. He's going to have to improve his draw a heap before he'll ever whip anyone worth bragging on. I suspect by now he knows this."

"Maybe so, but Miss Tillie says . . ."

"I wish folks wouldn't do that," Longarm said. "All too often they wake up sleeping dogs by going on and on about some shitty little spat that would better be forgotten. Not too many saw me back that self-appointed bad man down. So I better have a word with that doubtless well-meaning gal and see if I can get her to just drop it."

The copper badge said he doubted Miss Tillie would be on duty at that hour. Longarm didn't care. He had plenty of time to kill while he waited for those Indian Police to show up.

He parted friendly with the helpful copper badge at the next intersection, and ambled on to the Union Hotel. As he entered the coffee shop he saw the fat gal's place behind the counter had been taken by a slimmer gal. A far slimmer gal. There was much to be said for wasp waists and slender hips, but she was sort of overdoing it. He resisted the impulse to suggest she help herself to some donuts, a lot of donuts, as he politely asked for Miss Tillie, flashing his badge as he did so, lest she think him desperate to meet gals.

The counter gal seemed impressed. She said Tillie Beekman dwelt right upstairs in the Union Hotel, and they'd been expecting more lawmen to question her about those local bullyboys and that dreadful Big Casino from the awful outside world.

Not wanting to add to the excitement, Longarm simply got the room number he needed out of the fluttery thing and strode on into the hotel. Since he didn't know the day man at the room desk, and the sleepy-looking clerk failed to challenge him, he just crossed the lobby to go on upstairs as if he owned the place.

They still did owe him a place to flop this side of tomorrow noon, come to study on it. But he never went all the way up to see if anyone else was using the room he'd hired. Tillie Beekman had one of those smaller rooms set aside for traveling servants or live-in hotel help, down a side corridor toward the back. He figured a gal working the graveyard shift had had enough daylight snoring by this late in the afternoon. But he still tapped gently, aiming to come back another time if she was too sound asleep, or otherwise occupied, to be paying attention.

She wasn't. She came to the door in her robe of barn red Turkish toweling, the magazine she'd been reading in hand. As Longarm smiled down and ticked his hat brim at her, she went frog-belly pale and crawfished backwards, pleading, "Please don't hurt me, Big Casino! It wasn't *you* I was telling on when I told our beat man about those boys starting up with you!"

By this time she'd backed all the way to the big brass bedstead that took up most of her small room. When the pudgy gal landed flat on her back in the half-open robe, with her big thighs wide apart, it sure looked mighty silly.

He saw she had chestnut hair all over. He didn't see why that should remind him of old Joy's bare shaven pussy. But that had to be why they said variety was the spice of life.

Looking politely at the tintype of some other gal stuck to the orange and brown wallpaper, Longarm quietly explained, "My friends call me Custis. The only Big Casino I might take seriously would be another lawman they sometimes call by that name because it's a game he's said to be good at. His real name's Garrett, Pat Garrett, from Alabama by way of Louisiana and points west. After that we're both about the same height and build, with the same sort of mustaches. But that didn't give those kids the right to mix us up."

She couldn't have been paying attention. Opening her robe wider to expose a pair of downright amazing pale breasts, she sobbed, "Please don't be cross with me! I'll do anything, anything you want me to, if only you'll let me be your friend!"

Longarm chuckled fondly down at what she was obviously anxious to let him look at as he assured her, "You're making me feel a heap more friendly than I ever expected to feel with you, no offense. Do you want to see my badge?"

She was writhing about on the mattress, eyes closed and pink wet slit wide open as she moaned, "Show me anything. Show it hard. Just don't hurt me and I'll do my best to please you, Big Casino!"

He decided, "You know, this puts a whole new slant on that Attila the Hun sacking Rome. I wish you ladies would wait until us Huns, Goths, and such got around to *asking* before you gave in so enthusiastically. At the risk of repeating myself, I am not a gunfighting gambler called Big Casino. I am Deputy U.S. Marshal Custis Long, and if you don't quit trying to promote some sort of blood feud betwixt me and those pesky

54

young studs, I'll . . . I'll have to *arrest* you, that's what I'll have to do."

"You can't mean that!" she protested, sitting up to stare up at him, robe still gaping. She began to make a tad more sense, with her mouth at least, by insisting, "I was the one who *reported* your near brush with death. I wasn't the one who started it. It was that skinny brunette in the New York frock who started it, if you have to blame a woman for all that mean talk and scary gestures! I wasn't the one who encouraged that dreadful Krankheit boy to make a fool of himself, only to spurn him the moment a better-looking man came in. It would have been a mean trick if Lockport Krankheit had been a nicer boy with a sweet disposition, which hardly describes Lockport Krankheit at all!"

Longarm said, "I noticed. He likely noticed how thin the ice was getting under him, and by now he's made up swell excuses for letting me live. So I'd surely feel obliged if you could see fit to just say no more about what never really got going downstairs."

She'd recovered her senses, if not her modesty, as she told him in a calmer voice, "I'd hardly say they took it calmly after you and that dark-haired hussy left. My ears are still red over the things they said they were going to do to *her,* after they treated you just awful. Lockport said he was going to wait until you and a gal who should have known better were bedded down upstairs, so's they could get the drop on you while you were . . . you know."

Longarm dryly answered, "As a matter of fact, I did know. That's why they wouldn't have found nobody up on the fourth floor at all."

She heaved a little sigh, which bobbed her breasts considerably, and said, "They were really mad about that. Lockport vowed to find out where you'd taken that

55

brunette he'd seen first and make you wish you hadn't. Do you mind if I ask you something . . . personal?"

Longarm stared down soberly. "It ain't decent, or smart, to kiss and tell, Miss Tillie. How would you like it if someone was to ask me what you looked like naked and I told 'em?"

She smiled wickedly and suggested, "Go ahead. They say it pays to advertise, and everyone seems to think I'm just a durned old tree stump standing there behind my counter. That's the personal thing I want to talk to you about. I don't care what you did or didn't do to that good-looking gal! I want you to tell me how three hard-up cowhands could sit there within earshot, even ordering extra cups, as they talked about screwing and sucking with me right there, like they thought I had no feelings at all!"

Longarm tried not to grin at the picture. It was only amusing till one studied on it. He suggested gently, "Well, they've known you so much longer, as a counter gal, I mean, they may have just considered you a pal it was safe to talk in front of. That's another reason you'd best not keep talking about 'em with the beat men, see?"

She pouted, "Durn it, I ain't no pal. I'm a natural woman with the same feelings as that skinny brunette. I'd vow, and I've *tried* to watch my weight, stuck back there with all that pastry and long lonesome hours on my hands. Do you think I'm so fat I'm ugly, even . . . this way?"

He had to laugh, but tried to be gentle as he assured her, "You do have more to offer a gentleman caller than some, Miss Tillie. I don't find you ugly, though."

She said, "Mayhaps they'd have noticed me there if I'd looked more like an old witch on a broom or a bat-winged dragon puffing fire at 'em. It sure felt awkward standing there red of face but feeling sort of invisible whilst they talked about . . . What does a man mean when he says he means to give a gal a Greek lesson while a pal has fun in her old porch swing?"

Longarm gulped. "I'd have to know you better to even hint at what I seem to have saved that other lady from. Suffice it to say, I doubt you'd enjoy it either."

She lay back, thighs spread, to suggest, "Why don't you get to know me better then? I'm willing."

He blinked, more in surprise than dismay. "I can see you surely must be, Miss Tillie. But it's still broad day, we hardly know one another, and . . ."

"You think I'm fat and ugly," she cried. He put a hand to the door he'd never shut all the way behind him, trying to come up with a nice way to assure a lady she wasn't ugly without fibbing about her being fat.

He knew old Joy would be expecting him at that other hotel by suppertime. On the other hand he'd never said he'd be back a lick sooner. It was now around four-thirty, and . . .

"Oh, go on back to that skinnier thing and give her a durned old Greek lesson!" The long-neglected fat gal with the desperate as well as gaping love nest started sobbing.

So Longarm just shut the door behind him, bolted it, and warned her he could only stay a few minutes as she rolled back to her bare feet to shed her robe completely and dash over to bear-hug him so hard he had a time getting out of his damned duds.

The nice thing about a gal with such a big ass was that she didn't need any pillows under her hips to present her love-starved gaping crotch at a mighty welcoming angle. Human fat was funny stuff, if there wasn't too much of

57

it, in the way it gathered thicker away from where the bones rose closer to the surface. Tillie had far more gut than she needed to hold up her big old tits when she was upright. But she hadn't accumulated enough lard over her pubic bone to offer more than some nice firm padding to his own as he thrust his old organ-grinder home to the hilt in her passion-wet but tight-as-hell vagina.

There was no way any healthy man could have stopped in anything that fine before he'd come in it at least once. But as soon as he had, Longarm felt obliged to ask if he'd by any chance gone where no man had gone before.

She'd taken the delayed coming, inspired by thinking about Joy, as a compliment too. Hugging Longarm fondly to her heroic naked tits, Tillie purred, "You big silly. Did you really think a woman as warm-natured as me could reach the age of consent without consenting a lot? You should have met me when I was sweet sixteen and not half this hefty!"

He assured her he was just as glad they'd waited, since anything tighter down yonder would have doubtless crippled him for life, and rolled her over to put it back in dog-style before it could fail them. Her big white double moon made a swell contrast to the firmer and far smaller rump he'd be doing this with after supper, assuming he was man enough. But he was really pacing himself more to pleasure her body than his own. He humped her conversationally and waited until she was breathing harder before he casually said, "Lord, I'd like to spend the whole night ahead doing this to you, if only . . ."

"I can't. I have to be behind my counter downstairs, and I have to bathe and do some other errands before I relieve Blanche!"

So she never got to hear the grand excuse he'd just made up to account for where he'd be later that evening. It developed Tillie and the skinny one pulled twelve-hour shifts, keeping the coffee shop open round the clock. Better yet, as she began to arch her back to meet his thrusts, Tillie suggested it might be just as well if he stayed away from the coffee shop, day or night, until the threat from Lockport and the Miller boys died down for certain.

As he agreed she giggled and asked, "What's got into you all of a sudden? Or should I ask what you seem to be trying to get all the way into *me*? I thought you were starting to tire but, Lord, it feels like you're really enjoying yourself back there!"

He pounded harder as he answered truthfully, "I always screw better once I've gotten more sure of my fool self with a swell pal like you, Miss Tillie!"

To which she demurely replied, "I'm glad. I told you when first we met, at least a hundred minutes ago, that I'd always wanted to be your pal, and you do screw pretty swell yourself!"

# Chapter 5

Hoping old Tillie wouldn't decided she'd been sacked by Goths as soon as she'd cooled down, Longarm retraced his steps to the Ogden Jail, only to learn those Indian Police hadn't made it yet.

He went next to the Western Union by the depot to night-letter Billy Vail why he'd have to spend at least another night at that other hotel. Then, moving sort of stiff but feeling less awkward, he headed back to the Pacific to take that other gal to supper. He could only hope he still had the strength for dessert.

That was one of the more vexing things about woman-kind. Getting laid was a lot like waiting for rain. A man could go weeks without seeing a cloud in his sky or an eyelash batting within miles. Then the skies could open up to drown a man camped on the desert, or more pussy than one man could handle would come stampeding right at him.

Unlike some who kept a proud tally of their imagined conquests, Longarm had been let in on some female secrets, shortly after he'd seduced his schoolmarm—or so he'd thought—by another older gal who'd taken pity on an eager youth, or had wanted him to slow down a bit and not leave her behind.

She'd explained, and he'd never had cause to doubt her, that women were the hunters, not the prey, and that save for real cases of out-right rape, there was nothing any man could do to speed up the process of enticing a shy little violet into bed before she damn well wanted him in bed.

As that swell old country gal had said, and as Lockport Krankheit had found out in the coffee shop, many a man had the power to cool a gal off by saying something disgusting, or just saying too much. But given an amiable and not desperate way of acting, and assuming he didn't smell too bad, no man who was willing had to screw his own fist *all* the time. Moreover, the sweet little things seemed to have some spooky sixth sense about men who might not actually be drooling over them. This seemed to drive them *loco en la cabeza,* doubtless accounting for the deluge effect he'd noticed. He didn't even have to wonder how he would have have made out with Tillie if she hadn't seen him go off in the wee small hours with a better-dressed and better-built gal. He knew damned well what it felt like to order cup after extra cup from a waitress in a strange town in vain.

It might have been the contrast, but it seemed old Joy was even prettier than he'd remembered when he spied her in the lobby of the Pacific, hair swept up under yet another hat and wearing a lavender print summer dress this time. But he almost crawfished backwards out the door when he spotted the strange man she seemed to be talking to and heard the mean things she was saying.

Then she caught his eye, in a way that never told him to back off, so he ambled on over, hoping Joy wasn't making a habit of having to be rescued. For this cuss

61

was a grown man of forty or more, wearing an expensive made-to-measure frock coat with the ivory grip of a double-action Lightning peeking coyly forward from a cross-draw rig. Longarm packed his own double-action the same way, for the same reasons Hickok and other serious shootists had from the dawn of the six-gun era. Side-draw was a shade faster, although in only one position, belly to belly and afoot. But a worried man could get it out faster from more awkward positions from a cross-draw holster.

But the stranger in the fancy frock coat and tan Texas hat just held out his gun hand to shake when Joy introduced them. She said he was Stakes Slade, the roustabout boss of her tent show, and explained they were fussing about him having the damn show in the infernal rail yards, although still on wheels. It was her firm conviction they'd arrived too early, before she'd had time to make all the regular advance moves there in Ogden.

Slade didn't seem to follow her drift. He kept saying they'd used up all the time they'd paid for back in Wyoming and so their mutual boss, the show's owner, figured they might as well be set up and open for business, even poor business, as long as they had to pay anyone for letting them spend the night anywhere.

It made a certain sense to Longarm. But Joy insisted, "I haven't even had all our posters pasted up around town. When I wrote a check for the use of their fairgrounds I told them we'd be setting up on Friday."

Slade shrugged. "Write 'em another check, if they ask. Mister Palmer's going to have to write one for the railroad if we don't get out of their yards by midnight."

Longarm had toured by rail with the Divine Sarah. So he spoke up. "Wouldn't your circus train have to stay put in the rail yards all the time you were here in any case?"

Stake Slade looked less amiable as he quietly asked, "How long have you been in the tent show business, cowboy?"

Joy quickly stepped in. "You're not talking to a cowboy, Stakes. I thought I just mentioned he was the law." Then she warned Longarm to behave with a big-sister look, explaining, "What Stakes means is that there are extra charges for insuring and guarding a parked train loaded with people and their valuables. Once the cars stand locked but empty, the yard bulls only need to keep a casual eye on our rolling stock. It's up to our own security men to protect our freaks and finances over on the fairgrounds."

Longarm nodded soberly. "I stand corrected and vote with old Stakes then."

It didn't seem to make the roustabout boss feel any friendlier. Slade ignored Longarm to tell Joy, "You can take it up with Palmer if you aim to override me. I told you what me and my crew were told to do, and so now we're gonna *do* it. I don't care if the rest of you mean to put on a show or go for a moonlight swim in the Great Salt Lake. Amusing the suckers ain't my chore. I just set up the show, and I already know where them fairgrounds are so . . . it's been nice talking to you, Miss Joy."

As he turned and stalked off without even nodding at Longarm, the brunette sighed, "Oh, bird turds, there goes the lovely evening I'd been planning on! I'm going to be busy as a one-armed paperhanger in a wind storm for the next few hours, darling. Do you think you'd be able to hold out until, say, midnight if Mamma promised to kiss it and make it all better?"

Longarm laughed, a bit wilder than she thought the situation really called for, and asked, "What about your supper, and might I be able to help in any other way?"

63

She patted him fondly on the cheek, since they were in a public place, and said, "Haven't time to sup just now, and Stakes just told you how tent show folk feel about helpful outsiders. People who get in the way can get people hurt amid all the confusion of setting things up. So why don't we meet upstairs, in my room, around midnight?"

He said, "That's the best offer I've had within the last hour. But is there any law saying I can't drift out to take in the show, as a sucker, once old Slade has all his stakes down?"

She laughed and said she'd rather have a handsome escort home. She said he didn't need a pass to the midway, since they only charged to play the games, slip in to see the naked lady with a beard, and so on. She said, "I could give you one of my business cards and that might get you some discounts. But most of our concessions seem to be run by independent souls."

He said he'd noticed some freaks could be touchy, considering it seemed to be their own notion to expose their misfortunes to an unwashed world for money, and assured her he'd be content with the less expensive amusements. When he told her he'd once paid a whole two bits to see if a gal could really take on a burro, only to get disgusted and leave before the poor drab ever did, Joy told him they didn't have any really wicked freaks such as that with her show. She said, "Fixing the small-town powers that be costs enough when you hold it down to a roar. I'm can't say none of the girls in our troupe ever indulge in a little romance along the way. You'd just laugh that wicked laugh of yours. But Colonel Palmer won't allow any outright whoring. Fired a tattooed lady just last month for offering more than a peek at all her pictures for cash on the barrel head."

Longarm said he'd already talked to the local law about what a traveling tent show was supposed to provide, or not provide, in the way of entertainment. Then he said, "You keep talking about a Colonel Palmer. Ain't the show called Palmer and Lewis?"

She said the senior partner and founder of the show had died at the Great State Fair in Omaha just a few months back. She said it had been a freak accident, and that he'd been called Professor L.D.V. Lewis, the Wizard of Waterbury, which was a town famous for all the clocks that were put together there.

He could see she was anxious to get going. So he told her he'd heard tell of the Waterbury watchworks, and resisted the urge to ask what a dead wizard had been noted for, or what kind of an accident it had taken to kill him. It was none of his beeswax. So he told Joy he'd likely see her one place or another around midnight, and she said he was a darling for being so understanding.

After she'd run off to square things with Ogden, and put up some more posters or whatever, Longarm found his way to a chili parlor nowhere near the coffee shop where old Tillie worked. He ordered his steak rare, smothered with chili, and his coffee strong, with nothing in it to take the edge off. The Mex gal who served him wasn't bad, and sure liked to bat her long lashes. But after that last dumb salvo in Tillie, he could only hope, at best, to get it up again for old Joy, once he'd had time to digest all this red meat.

When he ordered extra black coffee to go with his double helping of cheese cake, the flirty Mex gal behind the counter must have read his desires wrong. Leaning way over, as if to show off that inviting draw between the brown rises under her low-cut blouse, she confided she got off around midnight and often left by way of the back entrance. He was still trying to come up with some answer that wouldn't get her sore at him when she added, "Is not so *discreto* for anyone but my *hombre,* Juanito, to linger here over coffee and tobacco long enough to make anybody wonder."

Longarm nodded soberly and replied, "I didn't know you was a married-up *mujer,* ma'am. But seeing you are, I sure feel ashamed of myself for drawing some of those pictures of us in my fool head."

When she demurely explained her relationship with a certain Mex railroad worker hadn't been formalized on paper, he gallantly told her, "That's all the more reason I'd best try to control myself. For you're the sort of *mujer* men fight over even harder when they only have death threats to hang onto her with."

She looked so pleased, he was surprised she let him pay her for his supper. But he did, leaving an extra dime lest she doubt he'd likely wind up jacking off over her, and drifted back to see whether those Indian Police had arrived.

They hadn't, and he didn't really want to jack off, or even play checkers in the ward room as invited to. So he asked directions out to those fairgrounds, and hearing it was a short ride or a walk a man in low-heeled boots could survive, he drifted out that way as the sky to the west was going from blood red to deep purple.

You could hear the tinny steam organ and see the bright multicolored lanterns strung above the midway long before you got there. More than one rig and heaps of riders passed him on the broad dirt road as he made his way across what seemed a burnt-off reed flat. The Mormon aldermen who charged for setting up on what they liked to call their fairgrounds knew a good thing when it was staring them in the face. The so-called grounds were simply unimproved flats nobody had gotten around to draining or subdividing as yet. A few miles off, the shitty once-sweet creek that watered Ogden and the Union Pacific sort of mingled in its smelly way with the shallows of the Great Salt Lake to form a duck hunter's delight. But since a dried-out duckless quarter-section or more of baked mud that was too salty for crops made as good a place as any to set up a tent show, yonder it stood, appearing open for business.

It took longer to walk that far across flat open ground than it did for the sky to light up with stars. But the stars got tougher to make out as you mosied in amidst guttering pressure lamps and all the sickly sweet smells that seemed to go with any midway.

That old Saint at the jail had been right about them not bothering with any regular circus events, although Longarm suspected some of those old boys standing about in clown suits might get acrobatic as hell if the locals commenced to act up.

The overgrown sideshow to the missing circus seemed a sorry sight to Longarm, who'd seen the Sells Brothers and P.T. Barnum's Greatest Show on Earth. But judging from the way young gents in bib overalls and young gals in poke bonnets were gaping about, Palmer and Lewis was thundering wonder enough for the Mormon Delta Country.

He didn't see anyone he knew as he drifted along with the gaping crowd. He noticed lots of them watched out front when the lady in tights who swallowed swords took a cavalry saber to the hilt down her gullet. But hardly anyone followed her inside, at a dime a head, when her barker allowed they hadn't seen nothing yet.

He understood why better than some of the worried-looking sideshow folks, he was sure, as he saw the bearded lady have even worse results. A dime was a lot of money to folks who'd just started to get their Zion in the Great American Desert on a paying basis. On top of that, he doubted even the wilder-eyed young cowhands or sodbusters knew what a Gentile barker meant when he intimated the bearded lady might take off that robe inside to prove she was really a lady. Boys or gals raised by the Book of Mormon took off their outer garments in mixed company all the time. Their Prophet had provided for communal living in often rustic surroundings by getting all of them to wear the same white underwear day and night. It was even cut handy for attending to calls of nature, or marital duties, without having to take it off. So naturally, few Mormons could be expected to be excited by the thought of a bearded lady standing there in long white underwear.

Longarm didn't feel it his duty to explain local customs to any barker. The local law was already concerned enough about unseemly doings, and that boss roustabout had already told him not to make any suggestions uninvited.

There was a somewhat bigger gathering around a brightly lit stand near the popcorn concession. As he drifted that way he heard a bell clang and a gun go off. It sounded as if someone had just fired at least a .45-28, rather than the .22-short of the sideshow shooting gallery. Rather than bull his way through a herd of excited strangers when at least one of them seemed to have an old army horse pistol, he strode over to the popcorn concession instead, to buy a nickel bag and ask the pretty little brown-headed gal who sold it to him what might be going on over yonder.

She looked sort of pouty as she explained, "New draw for that clockwork museum of Professor Lewis.

68

They reworked one of his automatons to draw and fire a blank pistol when that bell goes off. Nobody's beat it to the draw yet, but how could anyone but a total hayseed expect to?"

Longarm said he'd have a bottle of soda too, and pondered her words before he asked anything she'd consider dumb. He already suspected he knew why she thought the locals across the way were a mite thick. He knew what an automaton was. There'd been more of them about when he was a kid. The mechanical marvels of the Industrial Revolution around the turn of the century, mayhaps aided and abetted by that *Frankenstein* yarn by Miss Mary Shelley, had inspired a total mania for clockwork critters that did all sorts of tricks. Mechanical birds that sang naturally as any nightingale, or more human-looking automatons, a heap of them life-sized and mighty real-looking, to beat drums, twang banjos, and even draw pictures on paper with real pens and ink. For a time there it had looked like the whole business of bookkeeping was going to be stood on its head, the way spinning and weaving had been, by a mechanical wizard named Babbage, who said he knew how to compute high sums by machinery, if only he could find a damned machinist good enough to build it.

The fad had sort of faded by the time of the war between the Blue and the Gray. A famous chess-playing automaton had been exposed as a fake with a man inside, and someone else had pointed out how dumb it might be to pay hundred of dollars for an automaton to open a door or draw a bath for you when you could hire a boy for pennies to do that and other chores as well.

After washing down some fair popcorn with flat orange soda, Longarm told the gal, as if confiding, "Most of the really tricky clockwork ladies and gents would be older than you, or even me, by now. The most natural-looking ones I've seen were made in France about the same time the first Napoleon was giving prizes for fake butter, preserved peas, and such. The ones still about *do* seem to wind up as display pieces you have to pay to see."

He got rid of the poor soda, and dropped the bag of popcorn in the trash barrel while he was at it. "Never seen a quick-draw automaton, though. Most of the good ones were made before Sam Colt made that sport so popular. You say *they* rigged an old one to play new tricks, ma'am?"

She nodded absently. "Professor's daughter and son-in-law. Professor Lewis was killed last summer in Omaha. Before that he started this show as a museum of natural and mechanical marvels back East. It was Colonel Palmer who convinced him they'd be better off touring the country with all these extra concessions added on. Maybe they were. I never worked for the professor back East."

A young couple came up to buy some popcorn. So Longarm resisted the temptation to warn them about that soda, or to ask just how the automaton master might have died.

He put a bit more muscle into it to make his way through the crowd as he heard yet another clang and bang close together from that starter bell and blank pistol.

He was tall enough to make out most of the setup from a few ranks back in the crowd around the slightly raised stand in front of the show tent. The painted canvas rising in the lamplight as a backdrop was covered with printed brags and bright-colored pictures of doll-faced figures doing all sorts of things from standing on their hands to blowing bubbles. One of the troubles with automatons, as soon as you studied on it, was that the more real such a marvel looked, the less marvelous it seemed that it could do a task you could doubtless teach a barnyard critter to do.

The man-sized automaton standing near one end of the platform was more impressive than anything painted on the canvas behind him.

Longarm knew it wasn't really a *him*, but it sure looked like a natural man, dressed more Wild West Show than cow, in wool chaps, a black silk shirt, and flat Spanish hat that shielded its painted face in a way that made it seem real eyes could be peering out from the deep shadow of the brim as intently as the rest of the pose seemed to call for.

The clockwork gunfighter stood wide-legged but otherwise a tad upright for fighting, one hand out to the side while the other was gripping the holstered gun it packed side-draw in a tied-down buscadero rig. A vapidly pretty ash-blonde, down the other way, was presiding over one of those round brass bells you saw at a boxing match. As Longarm read it, there was a pull cord she tugged to ding the bell, while doubtless releasing some catch holding the automaton in position. The details of the mechanism hardly mattered. Longarm had to smile at how simple some folks seemed to be as the barker, most likely the son-in-law the popcorn gal had mentioned, made too long a pitch for someone else, anyone else, who'd like to try his luck against "Kid Clang," which they seemed to have named the dumb thing.

Longarm wouldn't have been half as disgusted if they'd been using the simple device as no more than an enticement to take in other automatons, which were doubtless far more complicated, inside the tent. But the brass-balled cuss in the seersucker jacket was asking two bits cash for the chance to win a hundred dollars by stepping up on the platform, face to face with Kid Clang, and beating him to the draw, fair and square, at the sound of the bell.

Old boys would either be dumb enough to throw their two bits away or they wouldn't. The fool didn't have to drone on and on about the late Professor Lewis putting together his clockwork kids, and about how you had to make sure the gal automatons weren't left alone in the same crates with the boy automatons. But he did, until finally one of the Mormon Delta boys piped up, "What if I was to beat him and shoot him in his clockwork heart? Would he die?"

The barker laughed and replied, "Lord love you, Kid Clang was never given any heart, albeit he's hinged to fall over backwards when he's shot. I'd be fibbing if I said that would really hurt a man made of painted steel, and you'll note there's a fair-sized backstop behind him to catch any bullets that miss. So how's about proving your brag, cowboy? How's about stepping up here and showing us how good you are with your gun?"

The local boy couldn't get out of it, what with even the gals in his party cheering or jeering him on. Longarm felt sort of sorry for the kid—*he'd* been a kid once—as the youth, wearing a Remington .38-40 and a sheepish grin, stepped up on the platform.

The vapid blond gal took his coin, more than two hours' pay, and dropped it in a bucket near her bell as she quietly told him to just relax, get set, and tell her when he was ready.

He said, "Hold on, ma'am. There's no boiler plate back of *me*."

The barker said, "None needed. Kid Clang is only going to kill you with a blank."

As he'd doubtless hoped, the young cowhand frowned and said, "Well, I reckon your clockwork killer's gonna have to outdraw me before he can kill anybody. So I'm ready when you are, ma'am."

The gal nodded, yanked the pull cord, and seemed no more surprised than Longarm when the bell clanged and the automaton drew and fired, almost at the same time.

The human challenger hadn't been hurt, of course, save for his pride, as he stood there, friends jeering, out a quarter, demanding, "Hold on, now! How did that thing *do* that just now?"

The barker smiled smugly and replied, "You said you were ready. But I'll tell you what I'm going to do. I'm going to give you a second chance. For one thin dime. One tenth of a dollar!"

The cowhand's friends seemed willing. The sucker who'd have to cover the bet with his own *dinero* grumbled, "Hold on. Your man has an unfair edge, with his hand already on the grips and . . . I'd like to know better how that holster works."

The barker in the seersucker moved over by his tin champion, saying, "I'll do this slow this time, with nothing up my sleeves. Observe we're not talking about a natural man with a human arm here. We got to make some allowances for the Professor's lifelike clockwork."

Kid Clang's right arm was bent at the elbow, they could all see, and the automaton hadn't reholstered the Schofield .45-28 all the way after blank-shooting the latest sucker. Gun muzzle and forearm now pointed down at a politer forty-five degrees. So Longarm knew what the barker was doing as he took Kid Clang by the wrist to force the gun all the way down, putting some effort into it, while his free hand coyly held the front of that spring-clip holster ajar. Longarm knew the metallic

73

snick he could hear from where he stood meant the simple mechanism was set something like a bear trap again. When the blonde pulled the bell cord, she likely pushed a rod with her foot at the same time to trigger the automaton from below with a series of push or pull rods. Longarm noticed the barker cocking the pistol casually as he let go of his clockwork killer. That would naturally move a fresh blank in place to fire. A stout fish line running to the Schofield's trigger through the hollow forearm would do the rest when the arm snapped all the way up before dropping back to its recocking angle. Longarm could only feel wry pity for a boy who'd bet another dime he could snatch cheese from a mousetrap as it was snapping.

The cowhand didn't seem as mechanically inclined. So this time Longarm was watching more closely as the sucker lost. It was a bit more interesting than Longarm had assumed, confused the first time by so much noise and black-powder smoke.

That Schofield snapped up and dropped halfway back, as Longarm had expected, but the noise and smoke never flared from the muzzle of what might be a busted hockshop relic. The loud report and monstrous puff of smoke—there was no flame—seemed to emanate from where the automaton would have had a belly button, if such creations needed belly buttons. Longarm saw why as soon as he studied on it. Such a mechanism would be far less complicated than the way he'd first designed the tin gunslick in his own head. Needlessly cocking a dry-firing gun for Kid Clang was a nice artistic touch. A pretty stage magician had once explained what they called distraction to Longarm, as they'd been distracting one another backstage. Cranking that arm down, likely against a mighty stiff spring, was the way you wound

Kid Clang up. His movements after that looked more real if nobody saw him being brought to life with, say, a crank up his ass. Longarm had recently read an English penny dreadful, put out by the same London printer who'd invented Deadwood Dick, featuring a steam detective who solved crimes mechanically for Scotland Yard. It was easy enough to picture such a wonder having to stop and restoke his firebox and take on water now and again, but Longarm had found it hard to believe a lawman running on steam could go on thinking as his pressure ran low.

As the smoke cleared, the young cowhand no longer stood on the platform. None of his pals, for all their rawhiding, seemed to want to lose any *dinero* of their own. As the barker began his spiel again, a copper badge Longarm had nodded to back at the jail joined him in the crowd to ask what all the noise might be about.

Longarm shrugged and said, "I'd say it was as lawful as a three-card monte pitch or a chance to see a genuine mermaid in the back. The dangerous-looking gent in the Spanish hat is supposed to be a game of skill. You win a hundred dollars if you can draw and fire faster than a spring trap can snap. But it only costs two bits to try, so what the hell."

"Why don't *you* try, Big Casino?" called an all-too-familiar voice from the crowd. "I want all you folks to see this! We got us a famous quick-draw artist from Wyoming here, and now he's gonna show us how good he is. Ain't that right, Big Casino?"

Longarm turned wearily to face Lockport Krankheit as everyone between them cleared away as if by magic. Longarm said, "I meant to send flowers when I heard your brain had died, but they told me you were still walking around too dumb to lie down. For openers, I am neither from Wyoming nor does anyone but you call me Big Casino. I am Deputy U.S. Marshal Custis Long, and while it would be a federal offense if you got lucky, I don't count it as all that much when I swat a pesky fly. So don't pester me no more and we'll say no more about it."

One of the Miller boys, further back in the crowd, warned the more flamboyant Lockport, "I think he means he's the one they call Longarm. I vote we say no more about it, hear?"

It didn't work. Lockport sneered, "Well I'll eat cucumbers and do other wonders if I ain't heard of you too, Longarm. I'm so scared I'm fixing to faint. But looking closer, I see you ain't twelve feet tall after all. Why don't you show us how tall you are by beating Kid Clang to the draw, Longarm?"

Lockport wasn't the only young squirt in the crowd who seemed to find that a grand notion. Longarm smiled thinly and said, "I save my bullets for bigmouths who annoy me. So far, Kid Clang ain't said nothing to nobody, Lockport. Why don't *you* take him on if you're so anxious to slap leather this evening?"

Lockport answered ominously, "That automaton never spoiled no other evenings for me. I know exactly who I'd like to slap leather with."

Longarm shrugged. "If wishes were horses the beggars would ride. I don't always get to do just as *I* want neither. They call such annoyances civilization. Are you afraid of that machinery, Lockport?"

The bullyboy stared thunderstruck and declared, "I ain't scared of nobody or nothing! I'll bet you anything I can outdraw and outshoot anybody you'd dare to name!"

So Longarm smiled pleasantly and said, "You're on, for a gold double eagle against a silver dollar if you can take Kid Clang."

Lockport grumbled he hadn't started out to gun any tin man. But even the Miller boys seemed to feel he ought to cover a bet offering twenty to one. So Lockport clomped up on the platform, announcing, "I'd be Lockport Krankheit off the Double Slash X, and I'm ready to take you *all* on, starting with this here stupid dummy!"

So the barker dropped his two bits in the bucket and told him to say when he was ready. The copper badge at Longarm's side softly said, "That human fool has real bullets in that six-gun."

Longarm said, "The other one shoots blanks too sudden for us to worry about old Lockport getting off a round."

The bully in the fuzzy-brimmed hat dropped into a gunfighter's crouch, gun hand gripping his own weapon, as he glowered and growled, "If *he* can start out gun in hand I reckon *I* can."

So the barker nodded, the blonde pulled the cord, and Lockport would have lost had he been a good loser.

He wasn't. Knowing in advance he seemed hardly likely to really die, Lockport ignored the blank going off before his own muzzle had cleared leather, and kept swinging his muzzle up, to aim and fire point-blank, setting the silk shirt of the automaton aflame as he fired three times to rock the clockwork contraption half off its feet.

Longarm thought Kid Clang was going over backwards too as he, or it, half spun on one heel to face the audience, shirt on fire and painted face glowing sort of satanically, and fired shot after shot out of the steel belly button just above its gunbelt.

Longarm had crabbed to one side and gone for his own gun without thinking. So the .45 slug that should have taken him in the chest thunked into a Mormon gal who'd been standing behind him as a man in the crowd wailed, "I'm shot! The asshole is shooting real bullets!"

Longarm was still acting more by instinct than clear reason as he threw down on the automaton, now exposed for what it was with half its duds and much of its paint burnt away from the cleverly hammered steel. Longarm fired, again and again, until the infernal machine was leaning back at a crazy angle, aiming up high above the heads of the crowd but blasting an overhead lamp to hot shards and scalding oil before its internal weaponry jammed, or it ran out of ammunition.

Things were still mighty noisy around there as folks just kept screaming, police whistles started blowing, and some asshole in a clown suit started hitting folks, yelling, "Hey Rube hey Rube hey Rube!" until another copper badge knocked him flat with a police billy.

The Ogden lawman who'd been talking to Longarm tweeted away on his own whistle despite the blood running down one sleeve of his blue uniform. That gal who'd been hit lay spread-eagle on her back stone dead. Others in the crowd, at least seven, could use a doctor bad. As two more copper badges ran up to the one who'd been hit, demanding to know why he'd called them, he took the whistle from his mouth to point at the thunderstruck barker gaping down at them from next to the shot-up automaton and yelled, "Arrest that son of a bitch for murder in the first degree!"

The barker protested he hadn't murdered anyone. But even Longarm had to agree when the wounded copper badge roared, "Well, *somebody* surely murdered this poor girl, and you *own* that dangerous toy, don't you?"

# Chapter 6

Things sure could get confusing with so many folks tearing over to see what had happened, while so many others tore off to parts unknown and that steam organ pealed "Rally Round the Flag" for no good reason Longarm could fathom.

As a paid-up peace officer, Longarm had to help the local law and security clowns restore order. It took the better part of the following hour to close down the show and clear the fairgrounds of all the folks who didn't belong there. A few who normally did had followed the owners of the murderous automaton over to the all-night police court in town in hopes of bailing them out, or at least to stand up for them before all those benighted rustics, as tent show folks were prone to consider everyone but themselves.

Joy had caught Longarm on the fly amid the confusion to say she didn't know how soon she'd be able to meet him at their hotel. He'd allowed *he* might be busy for a spell as well.

But things had quieted down on the fairgrounds, and all but a few night lights had been doused, when Longarm mosied back to the show tent of the late Professor Lewis for a more thoughtful look at Kid Clang and his fellow tin freaks.

The automaton no longer stood at any angle out front. Figuring the creation had either been hauled inside for safekeeping or impounded as evidence by the police, Longarm stepped upon and over the front platform to hunker down and light a match when, as he'd expected, he found the back side of the platform exposed, with about an eighteen-inch gap between the trampled grass and pine decking.

The pedal he'd expected stuck out handy to where that blonde had been pulling the bell cord. After that it got more complicated under the platform than he saw any need for. He could trace the rod running in from that one pedal a little over a yard. Then it seemed to get all tangled up with others, running every which way under there. When that first match burnt down he lit another, holding it further under the platform. It was sort of like sticking a lit match in the innards of a big old clock. The flickering flame couldn't say too much about dusty gear wheels and bell crank rods to a man who took his pocket watch to a watch repair shop when it wasn't keeping fair time.

A small shy voice asked him what he was doing. Longarm looked up to see that little gal from the popcorn concession across the way. She was wrapped in a chocolate-brown velveteen robe against the damp chill coming in off the Great Salt Lake so close to midnight. It was a couple of sizes too big for her petite form, but matched her pinned-up hair pretty good. He answered, "I forgot to tell you when I bought that popcorn. I'm a federal lawman, ma'am. Just now I'm trying to figure how come they needed so much clockwork to make that automaton move so simply. Looks like they got enough under here to make Big Ben chime 'God Save the Queen' with 'Yankee Doodle' thrown in."

She dimpled and said, "I think I can explain some of it. Before poor Professor Lewis had his accident, this pitch was set up different. The professor had a whole bunch of his children, as he called them, set up out front to draw a crowd. It was nice for my business across the midway too."

Longarm straightened up. "You mean all them rods and bell cranks had other automatons? Oh, sure, I can see the holes drilled through the planking, now that you've inspired me to look for 'em, Miss . . . ?"

"Rosemary, Rosemary O'Dowd," she replied. "The professor had them doing the most amusing things. I used to laugh and laugh in surprise. Because he liked to make them do different things every now and then. I don't know how. He was a nice old sport, but whenever anyone asked him how his dollies worked, he just winked and said giving away their secrets would spoil half the fun."

Longarm said, "Reckon I'll just have to let myself in and ask, seeing the present owners seem to be in jail. Would you care to show me around inside, Miss Rosemary?"

She skipped over the platform to join him with an enthusiasm that belied her casual remark about it being her duty.

As she did, she said that the owner of the entire show was over in Ogden trying to bail out his late partner's daughter and son-in-law.

As Longarm lit another match to lead the way into the cavernous dark tent, he asked who the present owners of the automatons were, and how the man who'd first put all this together had wound up dead.

81

Rosemary said Judith Lewis had married a jasper called Raymond Harmon, a sort of apprentice of the Wizard of Waterbury, after Harmon had toured with the show a spell. She said the old clockwork wizard had been sort of bear-hugged to death by one of his automatons as he was repairing it, or maybe teaching it to do something different. Nobody else knew exactly how the fool things worked.

Longarm found that easy to buy as he gazed in wonder all about them. He found an oil lantern, and lit it to shed far more light on the situation. He still found the late professor's mechanical museum worth the price of admission—if there had been a price, that is.

Weirdly lifelike ladies, gents, and critters stood or sat soberly all around. It was downright spooky to picture them all sitting there so expectantly in pitch-black darkness. He looked about in vain for the so-called Kid Clang. He saw a sort of cowhand with bright cheeks and an oddly sinister smile, standing on a sort of green box with what might have passed for a spinning rope if it hadn't looked so stiff.

Rosemary saw what he was admiring, and stepped over to reach around as if to grab the cowhand's ass as she suggested, "Let's see if he's wound up."

The cowhand was. You could barely hear his gears going round inside him as he grinned and proceeded to spin the frozen loop of his throw-rope, faster and higher until he had it spinning over his painted tin Texas hat.

Rosemary reminded him of a kid in a toy shop as she skipped over to a life-sized ballerina and got her to go up on both toes, twirl thrice around on one, and take a low graceful bow with both arms spread out real as hell.

The pretty automaton's skin looked real as well. It was likely something like sealing wax. Her dancing outfit was cut low in front, and damned if the results didn't look soft and . . . sort of tempting.

He turned quickly to take in the organ-grinder, complete with a monkey on a string, which Rosemary brought to life next. He didn't find the old cuss grinding the barrel organ all that ingenious, and of course the barrel organ would have played a tune the same way if a real man or mechanical monkey had been turning the crank. But the monkey on the string sure looked impossible, until you figured the string was really a hollow tube. And Longarm had to laugh as the cowhand went on spinning his rope and the ballerina kept taking bows for just a couple of quick toe turns to the tune of "Old Abraham's Daughter."

He followed in the young gal's wake as she moved round the overgrown toy shop, setting one monstrous wind-up toy after another in motion. He could see it made quite a show, and he found he'd started softly singing, in time with that fool organ-grinder:

> Well, we all march with the infantry,
> And don't you think we ought-ter?
> We are marching down to Richmond Town,
> To fight for Old Abraham's daughter!

That sounded so dumb he called ahead, "How long do these fool toy folks carry on like this, Miss Rosemary?"

She started a lifelike dancing bear to dancing, in real fur, as she explained, "I suspect their springs are way stronger, as well as bigger, than the ones they put in those German toys they make for kids to play with. I just told you Professor Lewis wasn't one for giving away secrets, but I know they can get all of these displays to going at once before they have to rewind any. Ray

Harmon is the one who winds 'em. Neither Judith nor me would be half strong enough."

They came to an imposing female figure in one of those barbarian outfits Mr. Richard Wagner liked his sopranos to wear, complete with long blond braids and a horned helmet. She sure had big tits under those steel soup bowls on her chain-mail dress. All in all she was a right handsome lady, who looked as if she could have made a fortune over in Virginia City on your average payday, hardrock miners liking their play-pretties sort of heroic but not too muscle-bound.

Longarm asked what the Wagnerian-looking lady did. Rosemary made the sign of the cross and said, "Nobody knows what the professor had in mind. This is the one that turned on him. Or broke his spine, at any rate. Ray Harmon found them in a sort of deadly embrace when he heard the old man screaming in the back and went to see what was wrong."

"What was wrong?" asked Longarm thoughtfully, as the realistic Viking goddess or whatever just kept smiling softly at them.

Rosemary said, "I just told you. It somehow grabbed him in a bear hug and hugged tighter and tighter until he was dead. Ray had a time finding the release catch when he opened her up the back. He said his father-in-law hadn't told him what he was trying to teach her to do when she turned on him like that."

Longarm moved around to the back of the statuesque lady in armor to see that, sure enough, there did seem to be a panel you could unscrew, once you brushed some long fake hair aside.

He got out his pocketknife and started to fiddle, muttering half to himself, "Seems odd even a mechanical wizard would be adjusting machinery you adjust from back here out front, where she could get at him. You'd best move out of reach, Miss Rosemary. I ain't no mechanical genius, and she's already made some sudden moves that surprised a grown man who thought he knew her better!"

He'd just gotten the panel off, to stare dumfounded at a total hash of mysterious gears, gear chains, and such, when a harsh male voice called out, "What's going on in here! Oh, it's you, Cupcakes? Who told you to fool with these automatons? Are you trying to wind up like Professor Lewis, girl?"

Longarm stepped further out into the light to tell Stakes Slade, "Miss Rosemary's with me, Mr. Slade. I asked her to tag along to explain these tin suspects to me."

The burly boss roustabout flared, "Oh, you did, did you? I suppose you have a search warrant, allowing you to trespass like this on private property?"

Longarm smiled wearily. "Don't try to jawbone about the law with a lawman, pard. This ain't private property. It's more like a public exhibition, licensed as such by Ogden Township, unless you're saying this show never had a permit to open tonight, or unless you have something else to hide."

Slade blustered, "I got nothing to hide. Weren't you there when we told everyone these grounds were closed to the general public until further notice?"

Longarm nodded soberly. "I ain't the public. I'm the law, trying to figure out who shot up that general public. I'd be proud to pay admission to the owners of this museum, if they were here to ask me. Meanwhile, I see the Ogden Police have taken in the clockwork killer I was hoping to find back here. So why don't we all just step back out front and say no more about it?"

85

Slade looked about, as if he hadn't been paying attention to the automatons before, and flatly announced, "The copper badges never carted Kid Clang off. I was there. I just came back from town with most of the others. The night court judge let Judy Harmon go, but he's remanded poor Ray over to the grand jury, holding him with no bail in the meantime. That girl who died was the daughter of some prominent Mormon."

"Never mind the victims," Longarm said. "Where in thunder is that contraption that shot 'em up? These automatons don't get up and walk away by themselves, you know."

Rosemary O'Dowd made the sign of the cross again as she shot a nervous glance at the big female automaton accused of murdering her own creator. "What makes you so sure?" she asked. "I've seen wind-up toys that walk, and Professor Lewis built these bigger ones ever so much more clever!"

The two men exchanged glances. It was the first time they'd ever been in total agreement when Stakes Slade said flatly, "Cupcakes, a clockwork killer that can shoot folks and then escape on its own is just plain impossible!"

Longarm said, "Improbable, least ways. Them walking wind-up dolls need someone to steer 'em if they're not to stride off a table or into the furniture. I've seen pictures of the closest thing to a brain a mechanical genius called Babbage was able to design, and it would have filled a hired hall, had anyone had the machine tools and skill to really build the whole thing."

The mechanical cowhand had let his rope spin down, and that pretty ballerina had taken her last bow till somebody wound her up some more. So Longarm said, pointing, "That just goes to show how long your average

86

clockwork killer would be able to get about on his own, even if he knew where he was going. How long have we been in here, Miss Rosemary, eight or ten minutes?"

She said that sounded about right, but asked, "What if Professor Lewis put stronger springs in that mean one?"

It was Stakes Slade who snorted. "They don't make springs that strong, Cupcakes. If they did, nobody would be able to wind 'em up. Railcars, paddleboats, and such all need a far more serious source of power because of their size."

Longarm had already figured why some called her Cupcakes, but he didn't have time to improve her mind, so he said, "Just take that part on faith, ma'am. The only way you could get a tin man to walk more than a few yards would be to have a real man inside him."

Stakes Slade snorted, "That's dumber than what Cupcakes just said. Me and my boys get to set these pitches up. So any of us could tell you none of these automatons weigh less than half a ton!"

Longarm stared thoughtfully at the large and murderous Viking lady as he mused, half to himself, "Ran into a road agent wearing steel armor, inspired by that Australian outlaw Kelly, one time. You're right about even steel *hide* being heavy. But detach one of these creations from its base, gut all the clockwork from inside, and what would you have?"

"Over two hundred pounds," said Slade, as if he was sure. "On top of which, none of these tin folks are joined like any suit of armor you could get inside. Those joints as move at all are hinged internally, with push-pull rods to either side of that hinge to move the arms or legs, and *only* the arms or legs, the built-in trick calls for."

Longarm swept his thoughtful eyes to the graceful gal in the ballet outfit. "I follow your drift. Kid Clang only seemed to move that one arm, and after that he shot bullets out his belly, which a real man might find sort of awkward."

The front tent flap swung open again and they turned to spy a man in a polka-dot clown suit, packing a sawed-off shotgun and a humorless expression on his unshaven hatchet face. He said, "Oh, it's you all," when he saw at least two faces he knew from around the lot. Stakes Slade said, "Evening, Luke. We seem to be missing that tin man who shot the Mormon gal. Might you have seen the police, or anyone else, carting Kid Clang away?"

Luke said, "Didn't even know he was gone. Figured they put him in here with the others. But what do I know? I just work here. Boss and Mr. Cotter are still in town, along with that Joy Hayward, to see if they can't talk the rubes into letting Ray Harmon out."

That reminded Longarm he'd promised Joy some midnight slap-and-tickle, and that he'd never make it back to the Pacific Hotel that early at the rate he was going. So he said, "I'd like a few words about clockwork killers with a man who winds 'em up for a living. So I'd best get cracking. I don't suppose either of you gents could suggest a faster way back than walking?"

The two men exchanged glances. Slade was the one who smiled mirthlessly and said, "You'd have to ask Colonel Palmer or Mr. Cotter, the pay and property master, for the loan of a mount. I just don't have the authority, see?"

Longarm smiled back just as sincerely and said he surely could. Then he turned back to the pretty popcorn gal to thank her for her help and ask if he could escort her safe to anywhere else she had in mind. So little

Rosemary blushed and allowed she knew her way back to her own sleeping tent.

Longarm didn't find it all that gallant when Stakes Slade tossed in, "She sleeps alone there. In case anyone around here had anything else in mind."

Longarm went on smiling, about as warmly as a wooden Indian in January, as he softly told Slade, "Don't push me no more. I've met gents I liked better too. But being a grown-up, I've learned to only push when I just don't care if it comes to shove."

Slade's beefy face flushed an unbecoming shade of boiled crawfish as he said, "If I was out to push anybody I reckon there'd be no doubt I was pushing, friend."

Longarm was aware a woman was watching too, and the asshole *had* called him friend, regardless of how sincerely. So he let it hang fire long enough to teach a bigmouth a lesson, then nodded and said, "Just so's we understand one another then. I was asking Miss Rosemary here whether she needed anyone to carry her home."

The popcorn gal dimpled sweetly at them both and said, "I can walk, and my tent is just across the way, you big sillies."

So Longarm said in that case he'd best get back to town. He had no call to say why he was in such a hurry.

The flat open expanse between the all-but-dark tent show and the few lights winking in Ogden at that hour seemed wider as well as more lonesome than Longarm recalled from earlier. There was neither a moon nor the usual stars to light the wagon trace he hoped he was following. Every now and again he'd step off into the burnt-short stubble of the intermittently reed-covered mud flats to either side. He knew they'd deliberately torched the summer-killed reeds that fall just as the Indians always had, to cut down the risks of wildfires, kill bugs that might otherwise winter over in the dead dry stems, and give new growth a good start come greenup. But it was still a pain in the ass, trying to make out the charcoaled stubble from the cinder-paved wagon trace in the little light shed by the overcast sky up above.

You could really smell salt in the air now. It was tougher to laugh at old Jim Bridger for thinking he'd found his way to a far-off Pacific when he'd wandered down out of the mountains to the east to encounter saltwater for as far as his eye could see. The Great Salt Lake was really far saltier than any ocean. But it also had beaches, salt flats, seagulls, and such like any other.

The reed flats this far inland seemed pretty firm underfoot at this time of the year. The stubble would make cutting for sign out this way a bitch by broad-ass day. But unless someone in town could tell him different, he'd have to circle that entire tent show trying come morning. For unless someone had carted that heavy automaton into town along this very wagon trace, the tin gunfighter would have had to have taken some other way, across a less beaten path to . . . where? And why?

"There's got to be a motive, unless the wicked human brains behind this clockwork killing are scrambled pointless, and even crazy folk usually have something eating at 'em *they* find sensible!"

Crunching softly along the wagon trace, most of the time, he went back over the killing a step at a time. Until he could talk to someone who knew better, he'd assume you opened Kid Clang, like that Viking lady, to teach him tricks and load the repeating blank-shooter in his belly. Since nobody had been shot with real bullets earlier, somebody had to have loaded a mess of blanks atop those last real army rounds in the spring clip, drum, or whatever. So Kid Clang had been set to put on his usual harmless show early, and to kill . . . somebody later in the evening?

"Makes no sense, save as deadly mischief," he muttered, pausing to light a cheroot for some company before he decided, "Had Lockport Krankheit fought fair, neither he not that automaton would have been shot that early. A bad sport banging bullets into a tin man who wasn't set up to get shot could have fucked up the mechanism and surely swung the creation in an unplanned-on direction. Where might that leave us if old Lockport had just taken his losses to them blanks like a sport and let somebody else have a go at that clockwork killer?"

It wasn't too clear Kid Clang had been set up to kill anyone by sheer chance. That apparent malfunction made more sense once you conjectured two separate magazines, maybe even two whole guns, with one fixed to fire harmless blanks when Miss Judith triggered it with her foot pedal and the other, under whose control . . . Or what if the trigger was a sort of breastplate, activated by getting slammed with a soft lead slug to fire a whole fusillade back at . . . another poor sport?

Longarm didn't see how anyone could have meant the death trap for himself or any other sensible adult, unless that odd way Kid Clang had turned to face his way . . .

"You're commencing to think like one of them poor loons who say they're Napoleon, with the British out to poison 'em," he sternly warned himself as, once again, he found his fool boot heel coming down on what felt like a dusty doormat over squish. There seemed to be more give to the reed flats this close to town. He hoped the drainage along this stretch was only run-off from those irrigated cornfields over towards the mountains. He just hated human shit on his boots.

Moving back to the firmer wagon trace, he thought some more about carting, or walking, a half ton of evidence away from that midway. Hauling it into Ogden would only work for some sneak who knew Ogden better than your average tent show folks passing through. Keeping that notion open but holding it less likely, he considered dumping the automaton in the Great Salt Lake, in any number of irrigation ditches leading over to it, or way out on the flats to sort of sink in and rust away. He decided that sounded easier than hiding anything as noticeable as a man-sized, nearly indestructible automaton in a town run by friends and relations of its shooting victims.

He stepped well off the wagon trace this time to feel just how much give there was to that charcoal-black surface. Steel wheel rims, or iron boots, would surely make deeper impressions. But he couldn't tell whether *he* was leaving any or not.

He hunkered down on his haunches for a look back at any heel marks he might have just made, lighting a match so he could shed some light on the subject. He couldn't see where he'd just walked. He could only hope something far heavier might have left him more sign to read some damned where out here by daylight.

Someone else, tracking by night light, had apparently spotted that earlier match flare, but hadn't had time to take careful aim. Longarm figured the son of a bitch had aimed well enough, though, when a rifle flashed about a quarter mile off and a bullet hummed directly over the crown of his Stetson, through the space his guts would have been in if he'd still been standing!

Snapping out his wax Mexican match, Longarm crabbed sideways on his haunches to draw and fire back at the second flash as that far-off rifle squibbed a second time.

He crabbed the other direction, away from his own muzzle flash, and leaped up to charge zigzag as he held his own fire in hopes of a better grasp on that bastard's position.

It didn't work. The sound of hoofbeats on soft ground told him he'd scared that rifleman at least as much as the sneaky rascal had just scared *him*.

He froze in place, out on the blackened reeds, head cocked as he tried to follow the hoofbeats with his ears. But the sly rider was safely out of range, and knew it when he, she, or it reined in to a silent walk across the spongy reed flats to Lord only knows where.

"At least," Longarm decided, "that couldn't have been no half-ton clockwork killer mounted on a pony!"

# Chapter 7

A promise to a lady who might be worried seemed at least as important as a suspect who wouldn't be going anywhere for what was left of the night. So Longarm dropped by the Pacific Hotel to assure Joy Hayward before he headed on over to the jail. He was about recovered from that afternoon orgy with the fat but frisky Tillie at the other hotel. So he was more puzzled than delighted when the brunette he'd expected to find upstairs was pacing the lobby, as if anxious as hell about something.

He saw it had been about him when Joy dashed over to him, grabbed him by the slack tweed of his frock coat, and sobbed softly, "Where have you been? I've been so worried about you, and we can't stay here, darling!"

He led her off among the potted palms, and sat her in a darker alcove to hear her out as she explained how she and the other tent show folks had given up for the night at the nearby jail.

Joy said most of the others were checked into that Union Hotel where she and Longarm had first met. She asked Longarm to go back there with her, and he said it might not be the best place in town for them to spend another night if they wanted to keep it their own little secret. Then he asked what was wrong with staying in the Pacific. She repressed a shudder and said, "I think someone followed me back here from that night court. Mr. Cotter, from the show, heard the funny footsteps too."

Longarm asked what sort of footsteps she was talking about. She said she and Cotter had agreed it sounded sort of like someone with big jingle-jangle spurs on, or maybe somebody dragging a chain. She said that Mister Cotter had shoved her into a doorway and turned back with his derringer out, to no avail. Neither of them had actually laid eyes on the noisy sneak.

Longarm said, "Well, we could hire a rig and drive back out to your tent show. But this sure is getting tedious, Joy."

She said, "Silly, we'd never get away with doing anything along the midway. Luke Blair is a notorious eavesdropper as well as head of our security force. But nobody will be paying any attention to our railroad cars, parked over in the yards and officially empty."

Longarm thought. "Ain't that likely to get us in bad with your boss, if the U.P. spots us playing house over yonder and charges extra for their own fun?"

She nodded, but said, "What nobody knows can't hurt us, darling. Mr. Cotter keeps the books, and he just escorted me to this hotel for the night. As to any old fuss working for the railroad, it's after midnight and I won't tell if you won't tell."

Longarm chuckled fondly down at her. "I can't think of anywhere safer than a place nobody else knows about. Do we need your baggage from upstairs?"

She confided she kept all the female stuff she'd need for the night in her private compartment aboard that train. So he led her out a side exit of the Pacific and along a dark alley. Finally she asked why.

He confided, "We've both been followed some this evening. The one after me out on the reed flats didn't jingle. So hush your sweet lips and let me listen to the night winds a mite from time to time as we circle wide for the railroad yards."

She did, and they did. She was a good sport about the bob-wire fence along one side of the yards as he held the strands apart so she could get through with her skirts bunched high.

She led the way from there to the tent show train, parked on a siding amid empty box cars, gondolas, and such. She naturally had her own key to the Pullman car, and they naturally locked the platform door securely after them.

She used another key on the same ring to let them into her small but comfortably padded private quarters. He'd forgotten how comfortably *she* was padded, despite her boyish figure, till they were going at it hot and heavy atop her bed quilts, the night lights of the U.P. yards showing her bare tits to romantic advantage as she bounced atop him sobbing, "Oh, Custis, I've been wanting to screw all day!"

He said he had too, which was only the simple truth when you studied on it. Thanks to old Tillie, he was able to hold back and let her come twice before he rolled her over to finish in her right, not caring how silly it sounded to groan, "Oh, Joy!" as he shot his wad in her, then kept on going, too inspired by the contrast between that afternoon and that night to stop.

There was something to be said for that Turkish notion of having more than one gal around the premises. It doubt-less kept a Turkish gent from pestering his neighbors' wives. For even the most fickle organ-grinder seemed content to grind the same old organs now and again given a change as great as this.

Joy giggled and said he was just awful when he rolled her on her hands and knees to hump her from behind with his socks on the rug of her perfumed compartment. He said she looked grand from this point of view, and meant it as he stared down at his old love piston going in and out of her well-lubricated cylinder. Fat old Tillie, that afternoon, had looked and felt entirely different dog-style, Lord love 'em both.

They finished right, and shared a smoke as somewhere in the night a clock chime gently told them it was one A.M. Joy stretched like a sleepy kitten, yawned, and suggested they get some sleep and then start again before breakfast.

He sighed and declared, "It hurts like fire to say so, and won't feel any better doing it, but I got to get dressed again and traipse over to the jail now, you sweet screwing thing."

Joy gasped. "Have you lost your mind? It's after one in the morning! Nobody else will be up and about at this ungodly hour!"

He answered, "Sure they will. The night shift at the jail gets paid to stay awake all night, and the prisoners in the back ain't as sleepy as one might think, what with all the time on their hands and worries on their minds. I want a word with that Raymond Harmon with nobody else about to distract me."

She protested, "He's not going to admit anything. He's told the same story over and over. We all heard him. Ray says what happened out there earlier this evening was impossible. Policemen who saw it happen seem to feel he has to be fibbing."

Longarm sat up, fumbling for the duds he'd flung somewhere around there in the dark as he said, "I saw it happen too. Leastways, I *think* I saw what happened. It all happened sort of sudden. I got me some questions to ask that others may not have thought of. After that, I got other fish to fry. Another prisoner and some Indian Police who should have made it in by now. So maybe I'll be able to take you up on that kind offer, and even catch some sleep, after I get back from that jail. I doubt it'll take me all that long."

She went on pouting and bitching as he got dressed again in the dark. He said she was welcome to tag along if she was afraid of the lonely dark. She said to just make sure nobody followed him back if her reputation meant anything at all to him. So he kissed her sweet and grabbed her spicy, and she let him out and locked up again as he sauntered off in the darkness.

He paused between some parked cattle cars to study the dark railroad yards a spell before moving on. He didn't even spot any of the U.P. yard bulls paid to drift about from time to time late at night. There was a raw chill in the night air now. So they'd doubtless decided they'd done enough about hoboes, who hardly ever climbed aboard an empty car that wasn't going anywhere for a good spell.

Back at the Ogden jail he found the night desk sergeant playing checkers with a turnkey. Knowing who he was, the sergeant told Longarm the Indian Police had hauled Kimoho Joe off to their agency earlier that evening.

Longarm said he was pleased to hear that, and asked if he could question old Raymond Harmon now.

The local lawmen looked surprised. The desk sergeant said, "I'd want to clear that with my superiors, Uncle

Sam. To begin with, the poor bastard's likely asleep in the back, after all the questions already put to him. After that, the killing he's charged with is a local matter. I fail to fathom how a federal lawman might have any jurisdiction here."

Longarm said, "A lot you know then. We could be talking about two killings, plural, one in Nebraska and another out here."

They naturally wanted to know more. So he told them about another automaton going wild and killing her master, creator, or whatever.

The turnkey allowed that yarn was worth waking the son of a bitch up, and led Longarm back to where they found Raymond Harmon not only awake but anxious to tell anyone who'd listen he was as innocent as a lamb despite his weak chin and shifty eyes.

Longarm had no call to sit in the cell with him. But he got out smokes for the three of them, there being nobody else back in that wing by now, and let old Harmon jabber on a spell as he got his own cheroot going. Then he said amiably, "I was there. Lest we have to pester your wife needlessly, I've already figured how she triggered the automaton after you'd cocked it by cranking down the arm and fooled around with that empty gun to make folks think those blanks fired from there instead of the belly of the beast. After that I need some help. That beast don't seem to be out there, and nobody can tell me where in the hell it might have wound up."

Harmon started to bitch about his property being stolen. Longarm said, "It ain't just property. It's the evidence that might serve to get you off or get you hung, depending. Before we get to whether it was designed for walking off by its fool self or not, I'd like to know more about the way it shot blanks out its belly button. Am I correct in assuming you load it with twenty-eight-grain blanks, as a rule, in some sort of internal Gatling gun?"

Harmon shook his head. "Hell, no, it's not as complicated as that. Kid Clang has this gravity-fed hopper up in his chest. Works like a seed planter. You were right about the way my cranking the forearm down armed and cocked Kid Clang for another shot. One shot at a time. I've no idea how it ever spun round on its rod and let fly that salvo of real bullets. To begin with, a full-length .45-28 army round would never fit the damned hopper. We tin-snipped it with just enough fore and aft space for our theatrical blanks to keep it from log-jamming."

Longarm said, "When you say *we*, are we talking about your late father-in-law and you?"

Harmon looked sheepish. "If the full truth be known, I was only a small-town machinist he hired as a sort of errand boy. He'd had this brain stroke and couldn't get around so good anymore. Needed a strong back and mayhaps a weaker mind to help him manhandle and wind up his creations. But I really did help him gut and refit the last couple of automatons he thunk up. Kid Clang and that other one that killed him."

Longarm grimaced. "Rosemary O'Dowd just introduced me to that bear-hugging Viking lady. Let's stick to the one charged with shooting up the midway and running off like that. You say your father-in-law had him doing something else first?"

Harmon nodded. "They all work much like music boxes. The mainspring slowly turns a drum, mounted inside what's more or less a big hollow doll. As the drum turns, it pushes different spring-loaded rods with its brass cams. It's the shape of the different cams in each automaton that makes it move different."

Longarm understood, sort of. He'd taken clocks and music boxes apart in his misspent youth. The turnkey said it sounded too complicated for him.

Longarm frowned. "Too complicated for Kid Clang, as soon as you study on it. If he works the way you say, he's only a glorified jumping jack. What do you need with all them cams and push rods if all he's supposed to do is raise one forearm and fire one blank before he needs to be reset?"

Harmon said, "I thought I just told you. The professor rebuilt him from an earlier, more complicated exhibit that didn't draw the crowds. You're right about the newer mechanism. We . . . all right, *he* froze all but that one joint in place by bending or removing a heap of the original rods and bell cranks. Using the old mainspring down below just to whip that one arm up and cock that rifle action inside would have called for retooling the original drum from scratch. So he just cobbled up some simple gearing and a leaf spring I helped him install in the emptied-out torso."

Longarm asked, "What sort of tricks did Kid Clang do earlier, and would his mainspring and master cylinder move his joints at all if somebody was to wake 'em up with, say, a bullet?"

To his credit, Ray Harmon shook his head. "Colonel Palmer already suggested as much to the police. I had to allow there was no way I could see that happening. To begin with, I doubt the mainspring could be wound any more. They all wind pretty much the same, with a big crank wrench, not a key such as you see on a wind-up toy. Them bigger springs are *strong*. After that, like I said, the professor cut or bent and jammed most of the push rods that had made the automaton behave as a circus ringmaster in the beginning. Some

101

of them rods, if not all of them, would still be jammed down tight against the cams so hard I doubt that drum could turn, even if the mainspring was wound all the way."

Longarm blew a thoughtful smoke ring. "Suppose somebody gave the whole shebang one hell of a jolt, and maybe sort of dented some steel hide and bent a stuck push rod with a lucky pistol round? You say the critter started out as a ringmaster?"

Harmon nodded. "Used to stand on a bigger base with one heel connected, so's the other was free to turn him around as he snapped his whip and pointed at the other automatons. The old man tried to fix him up to announce the other acts with one of those new talking machines invented by Professor Edison. But there seemed no way to make the automaton talk loud enough to be heard above the crowds along the midway. So after he saw nobody seemed impressed by his ringmaster, he came up with the idea of a quick-draw contest, since we were west of the Mississipi and so many old boys seemed to be packing guns."

Longarm had seen the crowd the automaton had drawn as Kid Clang. He nodded. "I can see how a creation designed to turn on one heel could do so unintended. Waving one arm with a whip or an empty gun while the other just hung still doesn't sound like such a dangerous notion. Let's get back to that repeating rifle action and some way to feed real bullets into it."

Harmon almost sobbed, "I've been over that and over that with friend and foe! There ain't no way it should have happened! Nothing but blanks would fit in that hopper. The simple action of a lever-operated repeater only fires once before you have to load and lock it by cranking that arm again!"

Longarm thought back and decided, "That arm was cranking itself a lot, likely moved internally by a push rod and a turning cam. As to whether standard-length army rounds would fit or not, I got to catch up with Kid Clang and ask him whether you could make a .45-short just a tad shorter by jamming the slug clean inside a brass cartridge."

The Utah turnkey objected. "You'd lose too much punch that way. The army-issue .45-28 is a weak sister next to a real man's .45 or .44-40 to begin with. The War Department's either cheap or afraid the kick of a serious gun would be too rough on their greenhorns. Remove even more powder to seat the slug deeper in the brass and what would you have left to fire?"

"Enough to kill a pretty Mormon gal point-blank," Longarm replied with a grim expression. "After that there's still the newer, more powerful powders starting to come on the market. Black powder's still good enough for me. Gun cotton can play hell with the steel of your barrels. But who's to say what anyone loco enough to telescope slugs into blank cartridges might use to load such unusual rounds with?"

The turnkey looked dubious. "You sure draw complicated pictures, next to simply having this prisoner lying like a rug. I know I'd never say exactly how *I* done it, if I'd done anything so disgusting!"

Harmon wailed, "I never done nothing! Why in thunder would a showman trying to draw a crowd inspire one of his own exhibits to disperse that crowd with a fusillade of freak bullets?"

The turnkey suggested maybe Harmon had been sore at the crowd for not spending enough. Longarm hushed him. "Let's keep some open minds till we can have a better look at that clockwork killer. You say the original design could sort of walk about on its feet, Harmon?"

The prisoner snorted, "Aw, shit, that's just silly! When it was still set up to move its legs it needed a rod up one of 'em just to keep from falling over. The professor tried to build life-sized automatons that could walk free, the way some wind-up dolls manage, sort of. The old man was pretty cagey about his secrets. Kept some from Judy, his own daughter, and Lord only knows what that big Viking princess was supposed to do once he'd finished her. But I know it couldn't have been walking about off her stand. The only walking automaton he ever got to work worth spit was that dappled pony you likely saw out yonder. And that one only got around, sort of, on four legs. They just won't stand up alone on two."

Longarm thought back. "I don't recall any dappled pony, or any pony at all in your show tent, Ray."

Harmon insisted, "It's there, I tell you. About three quarters the size of a real horse, with glass jewels on its carved saddle and bridle? You *must* have seen it. Sometimes, when the crowds are not too big, we put it out on the midway and let kids ride it."

Longarm shook his head firmly. "It wasn't there. But try it another way. If somebody put Kid Clang aboard a clockwork pony, and started it up, how far could it carry him?"

Harmon gasped and declared, "That would be pure crazy! Why would anybody want to do a crazy thing like that?"

Longarm said soberly, "I'd like to know why anyone would want a clockwork killer to murder Mormon ladies too. Let's stick with what someone *could* do, so I can catch up to ask 'em *why*. You were saying how far that clockwork pony could carry that clockwork killer."

Harmon looked flustered. "Shit, I don't know. Couple of hundred feet. A quarter mile at the most? You'd have to stick a crank under the stirrup fender and wind the fool pony up every few minutes."

Longarm nodded. "That would be a bother. But so would moving anything half as heavy as Kid Clang. Would this walking pony jingle and jangle as it moved about in the dark, with maybe someone less noisy moving beside it?"

Harmon shrugged. "They all make at least some clockwork noises, if you listen sharp. One of my jobs was to keep 'em greased so they didn't clink and clatter too unrealistically. If you overloaded the gearing, say, by asking a toy made for kids to carry a lot more, I reckon you'd hear some clatter, till the gears stripped completely. Why do you ask?"

Longarm smiled sheepishly. "I ain't sure. None of this has made a lick of sense so far. If I'm dealing with a lunatic who plays with wind-up toys, I got to consider things that don't make a lick of sense, though."

They jawed some more, till Longarm decided they were only going in circles. He handed both men extra smokes for later, and said he had to get on down the road.

It was far too late to pester anyone else in town, save for a lady who'd asked him to hurry back. So he headed for the railroad yards along a deserted street with barely a lit lamp in sight. The once-sleepy Mormon settlement of Odgen had mushroomed in the ten or more years since the iron horse had made it west of the Rockies, so most of the downtown streets were paved, and many of the walks were now slate or brick instead of wood planking. His boot heels echoed some between the dark buildings to either side. So he stopped now and again unexpectedly to see if he could hear any others out clomping around at this hour.

He seemed to have the dark business district all to himself. But as he neared the railroad yards he saw lanterns bustling back and forth, and heard some yard bull yelling. So he got out his badge and pinned it high on the lapel of his frock coat, lest somebody take him for a hobo crawling through their fence.

A burly cuss with a bull's-eye lantern and a baseball bat came over anyway. But Longarm had no trouble with him as he asked what seemed to be going on.

The yard bull replied, "You tell me. We heard what sounded like gunplay down this end of the yards. Nobody seems to be up to nothing, though. You're the first soul I've seen as doesn't work for the U.P. line, and I'll take that federal badge on faith. *You* see anything?"

Longarm shook his head. "Never heard nothing neither. I just came back from the Odgen Jail, which seems to be walled plenty solid. Might have just been some drunks further off. You know how noisy some old country boys can get when they go to town. I'm here to fetch something I left in that Palmer and Lewis show train, in case you were wondering."

The yard bull said, "Ain't no skin off this child's bottom, if you know what you're after and know the way."

So they parted friendly, and Longarm eased up along a dark slot between parked trains until, sure enough, he came to the Pullman of his desire.

He waited till he was up on the outside platform before knocking. As he was waiting he noticed the door to the car was not only unlocked but slightly ajar. So he slipped inside, calling out, "Hey, Joy? I'm back, and you never should have left the outside door unlocked like that!"

There was no answer.

106

A big gray cat got up and turned around a couple of times in Longarm's stomach as he thoughtfully drew his .44-40 and called out, "Let's not be playing kid games, honey."

When that didn't work he reconsidered how he wanted to approach a compartment door in almost total darkness as well as dead silence.

He dropped down to his knees and left palm, counted under his breath to a hundred, and after nothing had happened, crept quietly along the carpeted corridor as far as Joy's compartment.

He found that door unlocked as well. As he softly slid it open with his gun and the eyes behind it well below the level of your average man's knees, he smelled gunsmoke, a lot of gunsmoke.

In the shitty light he could see Joy was alone in there, up on the rumpled bedding, bare-ass, bless her sweet hide. So he got back to his feet, murmuring, "You'll pay for that, my proud beauty."

Then, when she still refused to answer, he lit a match, stared down thunderstruck, and groaned, "Aw, come on, Lord, you could have treated us better than this!"

Joy Hayward had been shot, a lot, with what looked like number-nine buck from both barrels. The worse part was that she lay there looking sort of tempting with her legs spread open, despite all the blood and the way she'd shit the sheets while dying so unexpectedly.

Longarm holstered his six-gun, and moved over to compose her dead limbs and cover her shot-up naked flesh with a loose end of the top sheet. Then he stode out on the open platform, drew his sidearm again, and fired three times at the overcast sky.

It seemed as good a way as any other to get some help, a heap of help, in one heap of a hurry.

# Chapter 8

Longarm had plenty of help, some of it left over from the Indian-fighting army and some of it grown gray hunting railroad yards for experienced hoboes trespassing. But nobody spied any sign, even after the sun rose dishwater gray but bright enough that overcast dawn.

By the time the county coroner's crew was ready to turn poor Joy over to the local undertaker her shocked boss had hired, her body was right stiff as well as waxen where the dried blood wasn't turning an ugly shade of overcooked liver. Longarm was glad he'd posed her more decently before anyone else got to see her. It didn't matter in the official write-up whether she'd been shotgunned in one position or another. Nobody asked what a lady might have been doing naked and alone in her own bed. If anyone thought it odd that a federal lawman had come calling on her in the wee small hours, they didn't see fit to bring it up. Anyone could see Longarm had reported her murder with his pants on and no shotgun near at hand.

A detective on the Odgen force, a middle-aged Gentile, allowed that few jealous lovers came after a lady with number-nine buck unless they knew well in advance she was fooling around, and with whom. He had a notion that the killer might have expected to find her there in the dark compartment with somebody else.

Longarm neither wanted to throw another good lawman off nor wreck what was left of a lady's reputation. So he smiled innocently and said, "The killer *could* have been expecting two for the price of one. When I talked to her earlier at the Pacific Hotel, she said she was afraid someone had been following her. So I escorted her over here to the yards, told her I'd come back to see she was all right, and mosied up to your jail to talk with Ray Harmon. About that earlier killing, out to the fairgrounds."

The detective said, "I know. They told me. Don't see how Harmon could be charged with killing that gal they just took out of *here*, unless, as some say, he's got some awesomely dangerous wind-up toys!"

Longarm grimaced. "Don't see how a clockwork cuss, even one who could walk, could see to shotgun Miss Hayward so accurately with no eyes. Harmon told me Professor Lewis couldn't even get the tin bastard to talk right. I'll be whipped with snakes if I can figure how you'd ever get an automaton to *see* anything well enough to aim at it!"

The detective suggested, "That Mormon lady out to the fairgrounds wouldn't have wound up any deader if the clockwork killer had been aiming or *being aimed* at her, if you follow my drift."

Longarm could, but said, "Might have been aiming at somebody else in the crowd, for all we know. That gal wasn't the only one hit. But we're just talking in circles, and I'd like to question some who might know more if it's all the same with you."

The older lawman agreed, and tagged along as

109

Longarm led the way to a lounge car to the rear, where some of the other tent show folk who'd been staying in town had gathered upon hearing the news of Joy's death.

Colonel Parkinson Palmer, who'd just arranged to have his poor advance agent buried first class, though far from home, was a big florid gent who looked as if he might be running for public office. He had on a fringed white buckskin jacket, worn over a sort of admiral's uniform, and a Texas hat. Longarm had already talked with him a bit up forward. Stakes Slade and that security man, Luke Blair, said they'd ridden in from the fairgrounds upon hearing the news. Old Luke looked more sensible out of that clown suit, but neither had anything to offer on who might have had it in for such a swell gal. Joy had been dead for hours before they'd even heard.

The vapidly pretty Judith Harmon just kept trying to choke herself to death on a tear-and-spit-soaked kerchief as she huddled in an oversized wing chair, red-rimmed eyes big as saucers.

Edgar Cotter, their bookkeeper and property master, was a few years older than Longarm but a good deal younger than the colonel. He was a nice-enough-looking cuss in a seriously cut frock coat the color of your average locomotive boiler or kitchen range. Joy had said he packed a derringer in that somewhat more cheerful vest of maroon brocade. When Longarm asked him about being followed with Joy the previous night, Cotter verified Joy's tale. He said he'd only escorted Miss Joy as far as the Pacific Hotel, and had no idea why she'd been found dead up in the Pullman car. He said he was never going to forgive himself for leaving her alone at the hotel after telling her they were both likely imagining things.

Longarm asked what they might have imagined.

Cotter said, "I thought it sounded like a drunk in Mexican fandango spurs. Miss Joy thought it sounded like someone fooling with a chain. But every time we stopped and listened hard it just stopped. I wondered if it couldn't be some trick echo, making our own heel clicks sound more, well, tinny."

Longarm demanded, "How come you suspected a spurred-up drunk? Were either of *you* walking drunk?"

Cotter looked startled and replied, "Of course not. I'm not so sure why I just said that. It was just a half-formed feeling the first few times we heard . . . whatever we heard. I mean, they weren't exactly footsteps. Not even spaced footsteps, anyway. Miss Joy thought someone was jangling a chain. I just guessed at spur rowels because I couldn't see why anyone would be dragging chains along slate walk. Can you?"

Judith Harmon suddenly blurted out, "It was *him.* I mean it. You have to let my poor Raymond out of jail. Can't you see my Raymond had no control over that monster my poor father created?"

Longarm and the Odgen lawman exchanged glances. Cotter told the weepy woman not unkindly, "Miss Judith, what you're suggesting just isn't possible. I don't know what your friend Miss Joy had following her last night. But it couldn't have been a tin man run by clockwork!"

Then Longarm asked thoughtfully, "How do you know it was following her instead of you, Mr. Cotter?"

Cotter blinked uncertainly. "I never heard a thing, or saw a thing, once I'd dropped Joy Hayward off at her hotel."

Longarm shrugged. "Neither did I when I escorted her from the Pacific Hotel to over here."

It was the detective who spoke. "Somebody must have followed you, Longarm, or figured out where she might be later. She never shot herself dead before getting rid of that shotgun, right?"

Longarm nodded soberly. "It's best to stick with facts you're certain of. Dreaming up extra details can blur the picture a heap."

"What was all that jingle-jangle about," Stakes Slade demanded, "if the killer was as capable of sneaking up on poor Joy unheard?"

Longarm swore softly under his breath. "I just asked you all not to *do* that. We don't know what Miss Joy and Mr. Cotter might have heard earlier. We don't know whether someone with a shotgun crept up on the poor gal like a thief in the night or arrived with a German band. If he, she, or it didn't have a key, Miss Joy unlocked at least two doors I warned her not to."

The Ogden detective gasped. "By gum, that's right, there was no sign of a forced entry. If she was shotgunned standing right in the doorway of her compartment by someone she knew, her body could have wound up back on the bed like that."

"We heard she lay naked," Stakes Slade objected. "Old Joy was no schoolmarm, but I sure can't see her coming to any door buck naked, unless she knew her killer well indeed!"

"Or he had a key," Colonel Palmer volunteered, taking out a key ring of his own to jangle. "Everyone attached to the show, and this show train, has at least a key to the outside doors. They're all fitted with the same sort of lock, right, Ed?"

Edgar Cotter nodded soberly. "Any number of people we don't even know could have found a spare or had one made. Speaking as property master, I've had to hand out extra keys on more than one occasion at many a stop along the way."

The detective said, "There you go. Say the killer used such a key to get into that Pullman, then simply knocked on the inner door of a lady . . . expecting someone else?"

Judith Harmon suddenly blurted out, "Stop it, stop it, stop it! Why won't any of you face the truth! We all know that . . . thing has a mind of its own. How many people does it have to kill before you let my poor husband out of jail?"

The Odgen detective smiled uncertainly at Longarm, who said, "It's up to your own superiors. I never charged him with anything federal, and to tell the truth, you're going to have a time selling a man locked up in a cell as the killer of Joy Hayward."

The Odgen lawman said he'd take that up with their prosecuting attorney directly. Longarm turned back to the ash-blonde with a weary smile and remarked, "I'll buy a twisted mind teaching new tricks to an old automaton if you'll buy it being made out of blood and brains, Miss Judith. Everyone I've talked to about him agrees your dear old dad was mighty handy with machinery. I was there when Kid Clang suddenly got to acting ugly. But your dad's mechanical puppets could no more steer themselves than a steamboat or this railroad train could. The first Indians who saw a steam locomotive coming at 'em thought it was alive with a mind of its own too. But we know better, and we have to keep our wits about us till we get to the bottom of all this . . . whatever."

Cotter said soothingly, "He's right, Miss Judith. The rest of us have had to move your late father's automatons all over this country, and none of us have ever gotten any good suggestions from a single one."

Stakes Slade nodded. "Lessen somebody winds 'em up, and turns 'em on, they just stay put like so many

113

statues. I've yet to see one move on its own, have you?"

Judith Harmon repressed a shudder and softly murmured, "Yes. It usually happens late at night, after the show's over and things have gotten church-mouse quiet. That's when you'll sometimes hear something creak in the dark, or spot movement out the corner of your eye. Raymond says I have a vivid imagination. But I asked my father one time, when I was younger, and he said real folks were only awesomely complicated machines, when you got right down to it, and so who was to say whether machines might or might not have souls as well?"

The Ogden detective signaled Longarm with his eyes, and Longarm followed him out to the end platform. The older lawman asked, "Well, what about it, do you think she's crazy?"

Longarm replied, "She's surely upset as hell. Old houses creak spooky after dark as their timbers cool, and who's to say a scared spinster peering under her bed is *loco en la cabeza*? I know it couldn't have been her grand design, or her husband's, to have a bird-brained bully shoot their automaton half off its feet by surprise and cheating. Ray Harmon says, and I agree, it would be a piss-poor way to drum up business, having your exhibits killing your customers before they could pay their way in to your show!"

Colonel Palmer came out to join them, muttering, "Poor little thing's slipped some gears in her own head, worrying about her new bridegroom. Isn't there some way we could get him out, seeing he has such a good alibi this time?"

Longarm replied, "We were just talking about that. But what was that about new bridegrooms, sir? Ray Harmon told me he'd been with Professor Lewis some time before that other automaton acted up."

The showman nodded. "Close to six months. My old partner hired Ray to help him as we were touring Ohio. But of course he had to court little Judy a spell before he got to marry up with the boss's daughter."

Longarm said, "Getting down to brass tacks. Did he marry her before or after her daddy got hugged to death by modern science?"

Colonel Palmer looked startled. "You *do* get right to brass tacks, don't you? They were wed a little after, and you weren't the first to speculate on whether my old partner would have given his blessings or not. But as in the case of last night's more obvious murder, Ray had an airtight alibi for the night Lewis must have been crushed by that automaton he'd been working on."

Longarm frowned thoughtfully. "Do tell? How come Harmon told me he was the one who found the body if there's proof he wasn't there?"

Palmer explained, "He'd spent the night in town. With a woman he wasn't married to, at a hotel where the night clerk remembered him as a big fibber. He wasn't married to Judith Lewis yet, don't forget."

Longarm smiled thinly and muttered, "Cast not the first stone and an albi is an alibi. The coroner's jury in Omaha was able to fix the time of death? Or might they have taken Harmon's word he found his boss dead when he showed up for work the next day?"

The detective from Ogden said, "I can answer that, Longarm. *We* check a prisoner's story too. Omaha wires that their records show the late Professor Lewis was stiff as a plank when he arrived at the Omaha Morgue before nine A.M. They agree Raymond Harmon was checked into a hotel, an hour's ride away, overnight."

Longarm nodded grudgingly. "Let's give rigor mortis

115

the usual four to eight hours to set in and let that Viking princess hug him so tight betwixt midnight and the cold gray dawn. Where was Miss Judith while her husband-to-be was playing slap-and-tickle with the other woman?"

Colonel Palmer said, "In their Pullman compartment up forward, down with the ague or some other female complaint. She's way better now, but for a while there, we were afraid we might lose her. She'd started feeling poorly back in Iowa. Spent a lot of time sick in bed about that time. What you're suggesting is monstrous in any case. Little Judy was my partner's own daughter, and they were very fond of one another."

Longarm protested, "I ain't accusing nobody of nothing. I'm just trying to get things straight in my head. Don't really matter where everybody else was if that Viking princess was really the one that killed her creator."

He started to reach for a smoke, and decided not to, knowing the Ogden detective could be a Saint. "I better have another look at that automaton before *she* walks off as well. Seems odd a man who put a machine together would be so careless around it."

Colonel Palmer nodded. "I'm sure nobody has any objections to you examining all the exhibits out at the fairgrounds. But you'd better do so today. For we'll be moving on tomorrow."

The Ogden detective said flatly, "No, you won't. Not whilst I draw breath and have a thing to say about it!"

Colonel Palmer wound up to argue, but Longarm explained in a less forceful manner, "He means we're in the middle of a criminal investigation, sir. It ain't customary for suspects in a murder case to wander out of the local court's jurisdiction before that case has been solved. And as of right now, we're talking about two dead gals here in Utah Territory, if not a third murder in another part of a federal union *I* ride for."

The old showman protested, "We can't stay here much longer. You gents have no conception of our overhead, and last night, thanks to the cheap spenders we drew before we had to close early, we lost more money than we would have by not opening at all!"

The Ogden detective seemed about to tell an outsider off for that comment on the sporting nature of his own friends and neighbors. But Longarm headed the spat off at the pass by saying, "You're perfectly free to just fold up all your tents and stay parked on this siding for just a few more days, Colonel. With any luck we ought to have things figured out by this time next week."

The old showman gasped, "Are you trying to ruin me forever? Of course we'll put on another show tonight! I've paid for the use of those fairgrounds and, what the hell, maybe all this publicity will attract a more adventurous crowd."

The Ogden detective frowned thoughtfully. "You folks assured our city council there'd be no hard liquor, soft flesh, or serious gambling, Colonel."

Palmer sighed. "I run a straight show when I *don't* have the Angel Moroni to answer to, friend. I'm sure I'd have a flashier show, certainly a more profitable one, if I turned a blind eye to some of the pitches who've wanted to tour with me."

Longarm murmured to the local lawman, "Palmer and Lewis has a rep for giving the sucker an even break."

The older lawman grumbled, "I can read. I just told you we send out our own wires. Did you think anybody gets a fairgrounds permit by persuading our city council they're out to skin the rubes alive?"

It would have been rude to say another lawman had brought the matter up. So Longarm didn't. He said instead, "I'll drift out yonder after I tend to a few errands here in town then. Got to hire a mount in case I meet up with anybody else aboard a pony, real or mechanical. And there's some book learning I missed growing up. So mayhaps I'll see you all again later on."

They shook on it, and Longarm dropped down from the lounge car to leg it back to the center of town.

First things coming first, considering how late in the morning it had gotten, Longarm scouted up a good breakfast. He picked the coffee shop in the Union Hotel, but not in hopes of an early romp with a fat lady. He knew Tillie would have just turned in for the day upstairs, and meanwhile, they served pretty good grub downstairs. So he ordered flapjacks and pork sausages with his chili con carne and black coffee from the counter gal with a skinny figure and a face a mule might have been ashamed of.

She flirted with him anyhow. Old Tillie had likely bragged on him to her pals. He was used to that back in Denver, and a man had to eat *some* damned place.

He'd finished his flapjacks, and had commenced to get rid of the cloying aftertaste with the spicy chili con carne, when one of the Miller boys, the older one, came in bold as brass to sit down across Longarm's table from him uninvited.

Longarm said quietly, "It's a mite early in the morning for this sort of bullshit, but all right, let's get her over with."

The Miller boy said, "I'm Tom Miller. Is it too late to sue for peace for my brother and me?"

Longarm shook his head soberly and replied, "Not hardly. You'll find me as peaceable a cuss as others

118

will let me be. I've found I get into all the trouble I can handle without making any dumb extra effort. Could I buy you some coffee, Tom?"

Young Miller said, "No thanks, no offense. Me and my brother Pete got to head on out to the home spread now. Just wanted it distinctly and forever understood we ain't at feud with any famous federal deputy!"

Longarm replied, "I just said that. Might you be hinting somebody else don't share your views on sweetness and light, Tom?"

The cowhand answered flatly, "I can only speak for my brother and me. It wasn't us you stole that pretty gal from. So we told old Lockport not to count on us if you was willing to fight fair, even before we knew who you was."

Miller got back to his feet, adding, "You saw how steamed the horny rascal was. He really cottoned to that black-haired gal."

Longarm said bluntly, "She's dead. Blown away by a ten- or twelve-gauge late last night."

Tom Miller looked sincerely thunderstruck. He sort of sobbed, "Aw, hell, nobody was sore at *her*!"

"You could be right," said Longarm. "They might have had somebody else in mind. Say somebody scouted the two of us to where I only ducked out for a minute, then told a murderous pal where he, she, or it only thought I was. Did you boys split up after all that excitement out at the tent show last night?"

Tom Miller didn't hesitate. "Everybody scattered once all that wild lead commenced flying. We heard later they'd jailed the cuss who fixed that quick-draw toy to shoot real bullets."

Longarm said, "Let's eat this apple a bite at a time. Were all three of you together when you left, and might

119

Lockport have had a pony tethered somewhere out yon-der?"

Tom Miller looked confused. "All three of us had ponies. Did you take us for sodbusters? As to leaving together, I never even saw my brother till we all got back together here in town at this all-night beanery after midnight."

Longarm let that go. Tillie would be able to verify that and give him the exact time, as soon as he had some time to spare her.

Tom Miller said, "Well, old Pete's waiting on me over to the Red Pony Livery. So . . . well, watch out for yourself, Longarm."

"I mean to, and thanks," Longarm replied, not asking more from a kid who was likely feeling torn enough already.

As he finished his breakfast, Longarm considered that Lockport would doubtless read about Joy's untimely death in the next edition of the *Deseret News* whether he already knew about it or not.

How such an asshole would take things from there was anybody's guess. A crazy-mean cuss was by definition unpredictable. It hurt least to hope he'd seen the last of a rival for a dead gal's favors.

Feeling oddly empty despite his hearty breakfast, Longarm went next to the Western Union, to find no reply to his night letter. Old Billy doubtless expected he'd head back to Denver without being told to, once those Indian Police took Kimoho Joe off his hands. So he felt no pressing need to wire Billy Vail that that had already transpired.

If he nailed a killer who'd struck across state lines, Billy Vail would be pleased enough about it afterwards. On the other hand, if he failed, nothing he was ever going to say could save him from an ass-chewing to end all ass-chewings. So there was no call to jump the gun.

By now everyone in Ogden who wanted to do business was open for business. So Longarm looked in the city directory, back at his own hotel, and found the name and address of a nearby patent attorney. Utah folk were whirling wonders at inventing stuff. It likely went with all the railroading, mining, and waterworks out this way. Most everyone had heard of the Mormon plow, and there was this young gunsmith who kept coming up with slick but simple actions for a new line of shotguns. His name was something like Browning. Longarm expected to hear more about the clever kid as his business grew.

The Ogden patent attorney was out of his office, gone to Salt Lake City to sue somebody about a water pump, his pretty young secretary told Longarm. She said she didn't know when he'd be back, and asked Longarm if there was anything she could do for him.

She had auburn hair, big chocolate eyes, and tits that reminded him of Miss Cupcakes out at that tent show. But Longarm knew she likely meant she was willing to answer questions and such. So he told her who he was and what he was after, explaining, "I know I can't check any books out here as if you were a library. But if you could advise me on the right books to look through, I might be able to find them at the regular library."

She made him tell her the whole story, sitting him down on a leather chesterfield before he was done, and once he was done, informing him he was barking up the wrong tree if he thought a clockwork killer made sense.

He insisted, "Professor Lewis was crushed to death by one of his automatons, and I was there when another one shot your own Miss Ida Foyle in the head out at the fairgrounds. I know somebody has to wind clockwork

121

up before it will do anything. But it might help me catch the . . . *masterwind* if I had a better notion what clockwork is capable of *doing*."

She nodded, and jumped up to climb a small ladder in search of a buckram-bound book on a top shelf of a bookcase taking up one whole wall. The ankles peeking out from under the hem of her blue gingham skirts and ecru petticoats were inclined to inspire his imagination as well. But once she'd handed him the tome, and explained it contained all the basic tricks of the Industrial Revolution, he forgot all about screwing her, even though he told her she deserved a big kiss.

He leafed through the illustrated tome on basic patents, like a kid in a toy shop, as she remained on her feet saying, "You'll find a dozen ways to spin a thread, run a seam, or tie a knot in it somewhere in there. Between, say, 1750 and 1850 some inventor somewhere had one of the thousand or so basic ideas. Every machine that's been made since before the war combines those original ideas, albeit in ever more original ways. I think we do have a book on mechanical exhibits, if only I could recall the title. Let me see now."

He went on scanning the one she'd already found as she ran up and down her ladder like a pretty squirrel. He found a whole section on cylindrical drums, studded with pins or wrapped in more cleverly carved cams, set to play a piano, fold and pack paper boxes, sign some lazy gent's name mechanically, or do most anything tedious over and over.

There was another section showing how sprung pins, inspired by punched cards or compressed air blowing through holes in a paper strip on rollers, could play longer piano tunes, tat lace, or even weave whole tapestries, with fewer mistakes than human fingers were

122

always likely to make. It was sort of scary to think of a big old tapestry loom ticking away late at night, in the dark, powered by a gently hissing steam engine with nobody watching as it wove artful pictures of unicorns and such and rolled them out of the way like it was . . . thinking.

The auburn-haired gal let out a happy little laugh, and rejoined him with a book written in French but illustrated plain enough for anyone with eyes and common sense to fathom. "Automaton" read much the same in both languages. The book was dated 1824, and there sure had been a rage for clockwork folks back around that time. Longarm had read enough regular history to suspect the desire to make artificial men and women at the time reflected the poor results of all the revolutions and utopian movements they'd been fooling with about the same time. There'd been all that fussing about slavery earlier in the century as well. So maybe inventors had sincerely thought to come up with a sort of clockwork servant class. For many of those early automatons had been dressed up like old-time servants and designed to do servile or just plain silly tricks. They'd designed whole platoons of housemaids, some of them right sassy-looking, to swish feather dusters realistically. The lady of the house, or a real maid, was likely supposed to move the mechanical maid once it got done dusting the hell out of one particular spot.

He turned a page, then quickly turned it back, sure the young secretary gal hadn't known exactly what was on some of the pages of this particular book. He'd heard the French prided themselves on being *pratique*, or practical, and he supposed screwing *was* a sort of tedious repeated movement when you weren't enjoying it yourself. But Lord have mercy, with a *clockwork* lover?

He smiled innocently up at the patent secretary. "These are just what the doctor ordered, ma'am. Just let me write down the titles, dates of publication, and such and I'll see if I can find copies to take home over to the library."

She said she doubted the public library would have either book, and told him she was sure her boss wouldn't mind him borrowing both, seeing he was a public official and all.

So he got up, told her she was a swell gal, and said he'd buy her a visit to the nearest ice cream parlor, if she wanted, as soon as he had more time and brought the books back.

She said that sounded swell. So they shook on it and parted friendly.

# Chapter 9

Back at his nearby hotel, Longarm shucked his hat, coat, and gun rig, lit a private cheroot, and reclined across the bedding to go over those dirty pictures some more.

The Frenchman who'd put the book together agreed, as best Longarm could read French, that dirty automatons were designed for a depraved sort of clientele by machinists who should have been disgusted with themselves. But since the book was supposed to be the alpha and omega on the subject of automatons, the author had felt obliged to include a chapter on mechanical vice, male or female.

It wasn't in the book, but Longarm found himself repeating:

> A dirty old man named Van Hue
> Designed a machine that could screw.
> Concave or convex, to suit either sex,
> And when done it could suck you, too.

As far as he could make out the lingo, one was advised not to lubricate rubber sex organs with whale oil or lard, lest they rot to bits or get all wrinkled and scratchy. Since he couldn't read the printed directions that well, it was likely just as well he didn't aim to fornicate with any clockwork folks in the near future.

After that, according to some of the pictures, mechanical whorehouses, such as they'd had in France back then, made a silly sort of sense when compared to making pretty little things do things like that against their wills. Pretty automatons didn't seem to care where a man might want to shove it, even if he was ugly or built funny.

The mechanical men built for screwing dirty old ladies tended to be built mighty funny indeed. Aside from being hung better than your average husband, automatons could be built to move impossibly passionately, and even twirl their dongs to literally screw a lady as they slid in and out, lubricated by some secret formula meant for pink or black or, hell, purple dongs of freakish shapes.

Before he could work up a real hard-on over such silly notions, Longarm probed on in search of any sort of automaton inclined to act as if it might be thinking for itself.

He found examples designed to do the damnedest things, with nobody controlling them directly like puppets on strings, although there was a chapter on glorified puppets as well. The Frenchman who'd put all this together seemed to agree that a self-contained automaton was more impressive than one operated by rods from below, although there was a fuzzy zone between mechanical folks with their punched cards or music box drums built into them and those with them down below in a stand, where more room might allow more variations in the repeated motions.

*Repeated* motions was the snag Longarm kept coming back to. By combining less than half the clever clockwork in the two books he had to work with, Longarm himself could come up with ways to get a life-sized figure to repeat the same lifelike movements again and again. But after that he was stuck. He saw how you might get a cigar store Indian to hand out cigars, or smoke cigars, or make rude gestures with cigars. It got too complicated when and if you wanted your Indian to stand there enjoying a cigar, offering a cigar to someone who stopped to watch, then snatching back the cigar and smacking the sucker with a tomahawk.

Blowing a smoke ring with his own cheroot, contemplating the exact motions he had to make with his mouth to do so, he decided aloud, "It would be easy enough to make a Romeo capable of giving old Tillie all she wanted in any one position. But asking him to roll off and walk out of the room, even slowly, would be asking way too much. Somebody would just have to pick him up and tote him, maybe while old Tillie wasn't looking."

Nobody had actually seen Kid Clang leaving that platform amid all the noise, confusion, and gunsmoke. Joy had said, and Cotter had agreed, they'd *heard* what Judith Harmon had called clockwork walking. Joy couldn't say anything more about it now. But Cotter hadn't said he'd seen anything, and had even allowed it could have been some sort of trick echo. You always heard unfamiliar noises in unfamiliar surroundings. Longarm could recall a lonely night when the shy sneaky sounds of his own blood, pulsing in his ears in the dead silence of a snowed-in cabin, had given him an anxious few minutes, followed by some sheepish laughter. Somebody doing something metallic inside any number of downtown buildings, after

127

the regular business hours, could have accounted for the funny footstep sounds a bit more sensibly than a tin man stalking after a couple and then not doing anything to them.

He smoked down two more cheroots, going back over that first tome, which only showed the funny ways you could make things move with gear trains, bell cranks, and slippery sliding steel. When you came right down to it, using a ball governor on an otherwise untended steam pump could almost be called thinking.

Paying even a stupid kid to sit and watch a steam pump by the hour lest it get to pumping too fast or too slow cost more than attaching a ball governor, which never dozed off or asked for a raise. Two sort of balanced cannonballs simply spun in a small circle geared to the main flywheel. As the flywheel spun faster or slower the spinning balls, spinning faster or slower, spun up or down on their vertical axle. That in turn inspired a push-pull rod connected to the steam pump's throttle. If it got to pumping too fast, the spinning balls told the throttle to shut down on the pressure a bit, slowing things down. But if they spun down too much, their push-pull opened the throttle wider, to feed more pressure and speed things up. The final result was a steam pump that thought for itself, at least as much as such a critter might be required to.

He'd read how James Watt, the wizard blamed for starting the age of steam and iron back in old George Washington's day, hadn't invented steam engines at all. He'd invented steam engines that sort of thought for themselves.

An earlier wizard called Heron had built a half-ass steam engine back before Sweet Mary had Baby Jesus. Others had come after, each making what was more like a machine than a toy. James Watt, as a kid, had been hired to tend an early steam-powered mine pump you had to turn a valve for on every stoke to make the big low-powered piston go up and down. Young Watt got to sit there yanking a valve cord every few seconds till it bored him smart. His first stroke of genius had consisted of rigging the fool rope to the machinery in a way that made the fool engine feed its fool self steam, as need be, at either end of its simple cycle. The mine owners had been pleased enough to promote the kid to head engineer, and all the other stuff about condensers, conservation of energy, and other shit had followed as the night the day, once Watt had simply decided a machine ought to do its job whether someone was right on top of it or not.

But Longarm couldn't find anything, in either book, suggesting how anyone with the tools and know-how of the age could build a clockwork killer that didn't have to be steered from close at hand. So what would anyone *want* with such a wonder? What could even a tin man with a better tin brain than old Babbage had tried to build do that any hired gun couldn't do better and far cheaper?

He put the tomes aside, put on his gun, hat, and coat again, and went over to the jail to see if they'd let Harmon out.

They hadn't. The Ogden law, having at least one bird in the hand, was reluctant to let the owner of that clockwork killer out before somebody told them where to at least start looking for the bolted-together bastard who'd shot their own Ida Foyle.

Longarm didn't bother asking to see their prisoner again. He was a lawman, not a defense lawyer. Harmon had doubtless told him all he knew, or all he meant to tell, and there was something to be said for a bird in the hand when you were trying to narrow a hell of a big list of suspects down.

He went to the Red Pony Livery instead. As a rule, whenever he was expecting to do any riding in the field, Longarm brought along his own McClellan, Winchester, and at least a few trail possibles.

Not expecting to chase a prisoner he'd been transporting, and expecting to do the transporting most of the way by rail, he'd taken a chance and, as was usually the case, regretted it now that he had so much getting about to do.

The old Shoshone breed who ran the Red Pony was able to fix him up at a tolerable two bits a day with an eight-year-old part-cayuse paint and a double-rigged roping saddle with one stirrup mended with haywire. A good rider knew better than to trust all his weight to the stirrups, so what the hell.

The old cayuse had a stubborn mouth when Longarm rode him around the paddock to decide. But when the breed suggested one of those Spanish bits with a rowel, Longarm said he'd rather just wrestle with a brute than bleed it weak. So the breed said he'd throw in the use of the saddle and bridle gratis for a Saltu who admired horseflesh as much as he did.

Longarm dismounted for the moment, and broke out two cheroots as he settled up in advance for a buck's worth of riding. As they lit up he casually asked whether those Miller boys had ridden out yet. The breed said they had, but that Lockport Krankheit was still in town, with his cordovan Morgan out back.

That had been what Longarm wanted to know. While he was at it he got the older man to verify what Tom Miller had said about the three of them getting in late the night before, well after someone had shot at Longarm and ridden off out on the reed flats.

It was a tad too early for another visit to that coffee shop. So he rode on out to the fairgrounds to see if he could maybe get a noon meal out there. It took no time at all aboard the paint.

But once he got there, there seemed hardly anyone around. As he rode down the deserted midway he spied some tent show folk here and there, but mostly off to one side, going about what seemed to be tedious housekeeping chores.

When he got to the popcorn concession across from the far bigger Lewis pitch, Longarm spotted Rosemary O'Dowd, dressed in a denim smock with her hair piled under a kerchief, cleaning the innards of her big sheet-metal popcorn popper. So he dismounted to ask how come they didn't seem to be open for business.

Rosemary wiped a strand of brown hair out of her eyes with the back of a hand full of cleaning rags as she wearily replied, "What business? We open early on Saturdays. But it's just not worth it on a workday like today. Who wants to pitch to bums who don't have regular jobs?"

He laughed and told her, "My job can keep me busy round the clock. I suppose you heard about Joy Hayward?"

She sighed. "Sounded like Paul Revere when that first rider tore in from town before dawn. Have they caught the fella who did it yet?"

He shook his head. "That's one of the reasons I'm out this way so early. Most of you tent show folk seem to be in town right now. Thought I'd have a look around while things are slow. Might you know where I could tether this pony for now, Miss Rosemary?"

She advised him to go on up to the far end of the midway and then keep going. So he did, found a stirrup-wide gap between a couple of tents that weren't open to the general public, and found a fair-sized rope corral on the other side.

There was only a handful of riding stock on hand. The kid who seemed in charge told him visitors were supposed to leave their horse, buggies, and such down at the far end before they got onto the fairgrounds.

Longarm explained he wasn't a regular visitor, and flashed his badge. So the young wrangler decided it was likely all right. As he showed Longarm where to store his hired saddle and bridle for now, the kid answered Longarm's question by saying that others connected with the show just hired livery stock as needed, as they toured by train. Since the show wasn't a true circus, they hauled no riding or work stock along from town to town. A horse could be a pain in the ass to anyone who didn't use it more than an hour or so now and again. Whether a brute was working or not, it needed to be cared for around the clock. That was likely what made new-fangled notions such as bicycles and streetcars so popular with town folks. The kid said all those tent show folks still in town at this hour would likely get out here for the evening show by hired hacks. When Longarm asked if the big boss, Colonel Palmer, had come back yet, the kid said he didn't think so. But nobody told him much.

Strolling back along the nearly deserted midway, Longarm saw some tarp-draped rides, that steam organ he'd only heard the night before, and what seemed to be some sort of steam plant on wheels. A big red box on a Conestoga chassis had a steamboat's smokestack stuck out the top of it. A couple of old geezers in

132

railroad overalls seemed to be doing something at an open hatch near the ass-end. So Longarm ambled over and introduced himself.

The old steam-fitter and his middle-aged helper didn't seem to care. They were pissed about the hard water from the fairgrounds well. The steam-fitter grumbled, "Damned Mormons say the *Indians* are a lost tribe of Israel. I distinctly asked if they were sure we'd pump soft water out here. Been operating no more than twenty-four hours and our boilers are commencing to scale. You can *taste* the mineral salts in the shit as you pump it. But what can you expect from slickers who call you a sinner for sipping cider whilst they frolic with a hundred wives!"

Longarm said, "I think Brother Brigham set a record with way less than a hundred, and last I heard, the Salt Lake Temple's been discouraging that particular revelation. But taking your word on hard water, do you gents power them rides, along with that steam organ, with this rig?"

The steam-fitter snorted, "Where else would they get their steam power? See that sort of duck walk running along the backs of all the pitches on this side? Well, there's tumble rods running along the whole shebang, like you see in a weaving mill, or laid out across the fields to power threshing machines and such. It's a whole lot safer with the rods turning over under cover, of course."

Longarm allowed he'd seen field hands torn up pretty bad by naked farm machinery, and asked if the engine that fed off this big boiler wagon might be in that big black tent at one end of their duck walk. The steam-fitter nodded and said, "It's a genuine Corliss hundred-horsepower. Want to see her?"

Longarm said maybe later, when she was running. He asked if it was safe to assume most of the show tents ran on their own power. The steam-fitter allowed they had to, a hundred horsepower only stretching so far. When Longarm casually mentioned the mechanical wonders of the late Professor Lewis, the steam-fitter smiled as if in admiration and said, "Old Professor really knew his onions. Didn't need no outside sources of power. He really knew how to coax all the power he needed out of those monstrous steel springs he had made in that town in Connecticut."

"Waterbury?"

"Yeah, that too. They called him the Wizard of Waterbury because he learned his trade there making clocks, locks, and wind-up toys."

The assistant chimed in with some observations about the dead man and his pretty daughter too. So Longarm handed out smokes and asked the quietly probing questions it took to clarify such situations.

But there didn't seem all that much to clarify in the end. The two old-timers seemed to verify all Longarm had already been told about old Professor Lewis putting together a mechanical museum back East, then joining forces with the flashier Colonel Palmer and more businesslike Mr. Cotter to tour the West under canvas.

They agreed that pretty little Judy Lewis had been more a decoration than a help with her father's mechanical marvels, until he'd had that brain stroke and wound up too weak to wind things all the way up with both hands. They said his daughter had helped, sort of, till they'd hired Ray Harmon, passing through his small Midwestern town, to tag along and give the professor a hand before his daughter gave her hand to him. Longarm made them go back over a few details just to satisfy himself there'd been no way in hell Ray Harmon could've planned ahead to run away with a tent show, murder his boss, and marry up with his daughter. The two older men who'd been there said Harmon had had an alibi for the night old Lewis had his accident, and Miss Judith hadn't married up with him until after the funeral.

Longarm decided checking what everyone agreed upon by wire would be a waste of time and money. He didn't see what difference it made whether every pretty detail was exactly right or not. He didn't ask if they knew who Ray Harmon had been shacked up with the night his boss had been killed. A man who'd fib to a hotel clerk would as likely fib to his pals, or even the law. It hardly seemed likely that that other woman in Omaha could have been connected with the show. Fooling with one gal you worked with and then marrying up with a second one could take fifty years off a man's life.

It hadn't been Harmon that automaton had been shooting at in any case and . . . Now *that* was something to study on!

Thanking the two older men, Longarm legged it down to the far end, where the Lewis tent stood forlorn under the overcast sky with a big sign saying "Closed" across its entrance flap.

Longarm entered anyway. As he waited in the dark interior for his eyes to adjust, he spied bright pinpoints of light, and eased around behind a row of silently brooding automatons for a closer look. Once he got there, he saw someone had made peepholes through the thick painted canvas. He got up on the handy box someone had left there, and peered through the top hole to spy pretty little Cupcakes O'Dowd slaving away at her popcorn rig across the way. The holes further down were likely meant for when there was nothing to stand on. You got a better view from atop the box. There was a sensible enough reason for wanting to count the gate out front a bit ahead of opening. Rosemary had just explained what a waste of time they found it to open for business with no business to be had.

He lit a match, and gazed about for something to light with it. A coal-oil lamp had been hung on a nearby tent pole. He dropped down to light it. But his match went out. So he struck another and, as it flared, noticed a sudden brassy gleam with one corner of his eye.

He lit the lamp before he moved over to hunker down and pluck the brass cartridge case from the dirt where the front wall of the tent touched the ground. The discharged and ejected blank had likely rolled under the canvas from out front. After that it looked more like an army-issue .45-28. It had "U.S. Ordnance" stamped around the center-fire cap. When he sniffed, the burnt powder reminded him of Shiloh. The army still used the same stinky but predictable black powder Du Pont had been using since the War of 1812. But naturally, anyone could buy overripe and hence withdrawn army ammunition sort of cheap from many a gunsmith. There were doubtless more cowboys and Indians than soldiers packing army .45-28 brass, thanks to picky ordnance officers and political considerations about fresh supplies from certain government contractors. It was only half-true old black powder could hang-fire or go off unexpectedly. Most of the withdrawn ammo fired swell, as Custer had doubtless noticed at Little Big Horn, with the Indians firing scrapped army repeaters.

He sniffed the spent shell again, and put it away in a coat pocket. He'd scout for more brass out front, in the better light, once he'd had a better look around in here.

136

He was just as glad Rosemary was across the way as, getting right down to cases, he hoisted the chain-mail skirts of that statuesque Viking princess to see if anyone else might have a sensible reason to climb up on her stand with her and hug her.

There didn't seem to be any. He silently took back some dirty thoughts about old Professor Lewis as he dropped the skirts back down the shapely but unpainted thighs of burnished steel and told the softly smiling automaton, "I was distracted by a dirty book in French, ma'am. Since I see you ain't that sort of a gal after all, just what in thunder *are* you supposed to do?"

She didn't answer. He didn't expect her to, at least until somebody wound her spring and started her up. He'd already peeked into the back of her shapely but all too solid torso. He hunkered down to find still another panel on the back of the big soapbox stand she stood on. It took some doing with his pocketknife. Once he had the back open, he saw a good-sized music-box roller with push rods up her right leg that likely moved all sorts of ways to judge by the bumpy cams wrapped about the big master cylinder. He saw some of the big steel spring down below, flat with the bottom of her base. That octagonal rod with a mess of tool marks was either meant to open a fire hydrant or wind her mainspring. So he went looking for some sort of tool to wind it with. The workshop he found on the far side of what he'd taken for the back wall of the tent opened up a whole new can of worms. It helped a lot that he'd just gone through that French book on automatons. All those body parts and oddly easygoing but awfully human-looking detached heads gave the confined and dimly lit space a spooky atmosphere. Thanks to that book, he knew most of the waxen-looking hands, heads, and such could be bought ready-made from the few shops back East that made the interchangeable bits and pieces of such wonders. There was a half-torn-apart, or half-put-together, cuss stretched out atop one workbench. He was supposed to be a clown to judge from his painted face. What he'd do once they put on his clown suit and remounted him on his stand would doubtless depend on the cams turning slowly under him. It was easy enough to see how a low spot, a high spot, or an in-between spot could inspire a push rod to move a limb this way, that way, or not at all.

He found a big steel crank wrench that looked as if it might fit that Viking gal's winding rod. So he went back out front to try and, sure enough, found he could wind her up easy at first. The cranking got stiffer after the first few dozen turns. She'd obviously run all the way down. It was small wonder she didn't seem to want to do anything. He wound her up as far as he could, and he knew he was strong as Ray Harmon. But try as he might and search as he could, he couldn't get the Viking princess to do shit.

He decided, staring at her from around in front, "That can't be it. Nobody would pay to see a big blonde squat and drop it. Even if they would, you'd have to *move* with all that clockwork inside of you, right?"

Getting no answer, he fooled with the slightly smaller and far prettier ballerina right next to the strong, silent blonde. He saw she had a similar cylinder built into her base as well. One he had her cranked up, he nudged the small lever he'd seen Rosemary fooling with the night before, and sure enough, the sweet little gal went into her tedious but pretty enough ballet dance. When she ended with that swanlike bow and straightened up to wait and see if he wanted her to do it again, he had a sudden thought he was a tad ashamed of, but what the hell.

It was easy enough to pull down the French under-drawers of a gal in such a scandalous little skirt, and sure enough, she'd been made far more realistically than the big blonde on the other stand. There was no pubic hair, and the soft red rubber lips of her artificial pussy pouted more forward than a real gal's might have. But many a man had noticed nature had designed real women a tad awkward for a man to get *at,* and someone had obviously been out to improve on nature here, or at least *match* it!

Leaving the oddly colored but soft and smooth artificial privates exposed, Longarm started the ballerina up again and watched, with a bemused expression and some experience in carnal matters, as the tin lady calmly went into her ballet routine with her lacy underdrawers down around one trim ankle. Some of the poses she struck were bawdy indeed, but when she twirled on tiptoe he decided, "That's just not the way even dirty old Van Hue would want a clockwork screwer to screw. A sex maniac would be better off with a big rubber dolly that held still. So why go to so much trouble just to . . ."

He nodded, moved over to the Viking princess, and hunkered down to see if her master cylinder came out. It did, once you found the right way to turn some retaining screws. By the time he had it out the ballerina had quit dancing again. So he removed her glorified music-box drum and then he switched both, putting each gal's mess of clever cams in the base of the other.

The Viking princess still didn't want to do shit. He figured it had to be that she was planted solid, on both feet. It only stood to reason that directions to stand up on one toe and spin around would simply result in a jammed drum.

The results of starting up that other drum in the base of the ballerina were more interesting. Longarm gasped, "Hidden in plain sight, like that purloined letter in that tale by Mister Poe!" as the innocently smiling little ballerina put her hands up behind her head, thrust her hips forward with her shapely thighs well apart, and proceeded to bump and grind in a manner to excite even a man who knew better!

Longarm marveled, "Jesus H. Christ, if old Tillie could move like that she'd be married by now, fat as she might be! Professor Lewis was a widower, and dirty old men have natural feelings too. So right, this had to be at least as decent a solution as incest with his not-much-better-looking daughter. But I can see how such habits could lead to a brain stroke, ma'am."

The wickedly moving automaton went on bumping and grinding at him in a manner designed to make any man at least a tad curious. Longarm wasn't about to stick his own dong, or even a finger, into Lord only knows what. But he didn't think a clockwork gal would feel discomfort if he poked her with a crank handle to see how far up she might go inside.

It was a good thing for him he'd been so fastidious. The smooth rounded handle of the winding tool, much the same size and shape as an average man's pecker, slid up into the gyrating vagina in a way that felt tempting as hell. But when Longarm slid it deeper, feeling stupid, and feeling a dull click when he hit bottom, those two upraised arms snapped down across the automaton's shapely chest with as much force, and mercy, as a sprung bear trap!

"Holy shit!" gasped Longarm from where he'd landed, six or eight feet away, as the automaton kept bumping and grinding, a steel crank up her snatch, as she hugged

140

the hell out of nobody at all with her thin metal arms.

"Now I know Professor Lewis never designed you to do *that*!" he decided, even as the life-sized love toy ran down to just coyly hug nobody at all to her metal breasts, at least this time.

He pulled her underdrawers back up, confiding, "We'll just put both you ladies back the other way for now, lest somebody meaner suspect I'm getting warmer."

As he changed cylinders, he could think of two ways a dirty but dead old man could have been found in the arms of that other clockwork gal. Somebody could have moved his body afterwards, or somebody could have changed the wigs and duds of the neighboring and not too otherwise different-looking automatons.

He tried removing the Viking helmet and blond hair. When they both lifted off, exposing a smooth-painted scalp, he put them back, muttering, "Somebody sure has gone to a whole heap of sneaky skullduggery for *some* damned reason!"

He knew that the real reason was all he needed to make some damned arrests around here, now that he was more certain it was a matter of at least two killings across more than one state line.

# Chapter 10

Rosemary O'Dowd had finished cleaning and setting up for that evening's gate by the time Longarm had found the box of theatrical blanks under a worktable. So she wandered across the midway while he was probing about on his hands and knees between the platform and tent walls out front. When she asked what he was doing, Longarm got back to his feet with a weary smile and explained, "I thought I was hunting for more empty brass. But I see somebody must have got here before me."

She looked so confounded he stepped up on the platform with her to hold up two shells between the same thumb and forefinger as he said, "I helped myself to the shorter theatrical blank in the back, where Ray Harmon doubtless loads that magazine of Kid Clang. When you pry out the waxed wadding you find black powder with sprinkles of what looks like photo-flash magnesium to get more flash-bang for the buck. The blank brass is stamped Peters. That's a big Eastern firm that makes lots of affordable ammo. This army shell is heavier brass, made to bang more seriously. It smells as if it was loaded the regular way with regular powder, giving it a good enough punch for casual killing. It's a tad longer than the blank. So even with its slug telescoped down atop more powerful gun cotton, it wouldn't fit in Kid Clang's magazine, if Ray Harmon knows what he's talking about."

She said she wished she understood what *he* was talking about. So Longarm told her, "I wish I did too. Every time I get a grand notion I seem to cut sign that leads me down another trail entirely! It had just occurred to me that without that mulish Lockport Krankheit's cheating last night, that young Mormon gal might still be alive. But let's not be too hasty about Ray Harmon."

He pointed at the far end of the platform, where Harmon had been barking, as he elaborated. "Say the quick-draw automaton would be standing right about where you are, spitting blanks that way, up the line towards each and every challenger. Where would Harmon be the moment Kid Clang opened fire with real bullets?"

Rosemary stared uncertainly at nobody, trying to repopulate the platform with the figures upon it the night before, and suddenly gasped, "Good heavens! There's that backstop behind me, but not a thing to catch bullets flying the other way!"

Longarm nodded soberly. "Harmon doubtless felt no need of one, just to stop flash, bang, and maybe a little wadding that would hardly carry the length of this platform. But let's say that clockwork quick-draw artist was set up to fire blanks for a spell and then open up with a whole fusillade of rapid-fire .45-28. Well, both Lockport Krankheit and the barker directly behind him could have wound up as dead as Miss Ida Foyle did when Lockport spun the automaton her way with his own wild fusillade!"

Rosemary gasped, "Good Lord! Then poor Ray Harmon was the real killer's intended target!"

She'd sounded more certain than Longarm, who complained, "I just said I was having a time making things fit right. Harmon insists a .45-28 just won't fire out of that fool clockwork killer. Unless he was out to commit suicide last night, I have no call to argue that point with him. It was his automaton. It was aimed at him until just before it started shooting, but how?"

She asked, "What about that gun it had in its hand? Wasn't that a regular old army .45?"

He nodded thoughtfully. "Schofield Colt .45-28 out of some junk shop. Junky old guns are mean enough, at close range, but Harmon said that was only misdirection and that the handgun wasn't rigged to really fire."

Rosemary shrugged. "Would someone out to kill a man tell him there'd been a slight change in plans?"

Longarm laughed down at her and declared, "I just found another automaton rigged to act sort of unusual inside. You'd make a swell tracker, Miss Rosemary. You think sneaky enough. Is there somewheres around here we could have a sit-down talk over coffee or even your noon dinner? I'd be proud to pay for both of us, and I want to know what else you can suggest about sneaky doings out this way!"

She said none of the food stands were open yet, even if he thought she was careless enough to eat fairgrounds grub. Then she suggested they have scrambled eggs at her tent, if he could go for that instead of pickled pigs feet or candied apples.

He said scrambled eggs sounded healthier. So she led him across the way, beyond her popcorn concession, to an old army squad tent repainted barn red. Inside, she had it fixed up with a camp stove, army cot, and other portable furnishings, to use as her home away from the railroad tracks, on a rainy day or after hours with that train an inconvenient haul away in the dark.

She sat him on her cot, and got to work at her camp stove, which ran on coal oil, once she'd used up half a dozen matches and some unladylike words that wouldn't have really upset a mule skinner.

As she put on the pot and whipped up some eggs with chopped onions and bell peppers, he got more out of her about who might have been doing what, with whom, or to whom, of late. She said she didn't know who Ray Harmon had been sparking before he'd suddenly married up with Judith Lewis. She assumed he'd been sparking somebody because, in all modesty, most of the men with the show who didn't have anyone else seemed leather-bent on finding out whether her own so-called cupcakes were real or not.

When he asked her if they were, she shot him a roguish grin over one shoulder to say that was for her to know and him to find out. But he asked, "Might you have heard whether Professor Lewis or Ray Harmon had taken out serious life-insurance policies, Miss Rosemary?"

She said, "You *do* think sneaky, don't you? I can't say about Ray. You never know whether a man has life insurance or not until he dies, and even then some fib. I know the professor died in his testicles and left his daughter mostly past-due bills. Seems he'd cashed in the insurance she'd thought he had to buy more clockwork, costumes, wigs, and such. Sometimes he acted as if those automatons meant more to him than real kith and kin."

Longarm said, "I think *intestate* is the word for dying broke. Miss Judith told me she used to hear funny noises

145

in the dark after they'd shut down for the night. But hold on, wasn't Professor Lewis part owner of this whole shebang?"

Rosemary brought their tray over to her cot so they could eat from it side by side, saying, "Coffee will be ready by the time you finish those eggs. Judy and her husband are only junior partners now. She had to sell some of her shares to Colonel Palmer in order to pay off the swamping debts her inventive dad left her. You could ask Mr. Cotter for the exact details. I only heard them talking about it in bits and pieces from time to time. Mr. Cotter took care of the paperwork. As for owning any shares in this fool show, it hasn't shown a profit for months. Those of us with concessions but no say in the management or bookings pay the ownership for such room as we take up on the train or on grounds the management pays the rubes to use. After that we're supposed to pay ten percent of our net nut. Which in my case, at least, comes to next to nothing. I didn't make enough to pay for expenses last night, and it looks like rain by sundown!"

He swallowed and said soothingly, "You make swell eggs, and it's hard to say about fall weather along the shores of the Great Salt Lake. Surely a poor gate one place evens out with a good showing at the next, though, right?"

She got up to check the pot. "If only. I swear to God I couldn't book this show into more hick towns inhabited by poor folk, skinflints, or both, with an atlas and a really bad streak of stupidity. I'm not the only one who's begged the colonel to swung back to the eastern states, where the towns are closer together and the crowds are bigger. But he's as stubborn about that as he is about wheels of fortune and geeks."

146

As she handed Longarm his cup of coffee he nodded his thanks and said, "Everyone agrees he runs a straighter show than most. I find a geek swallowing live rats or biting the heads off chickens sort of disgusting, and I know for a fact that serious gambling can lead to shootouts between show and town folk."

She looked away and said, "I know. My man, Frank, was stabbed in a hey-rube in Pennsylvania when we were traveling with the Barnum sideshow. But serious gambling still brings serious money to the midway, and sports who've just seen someone win or lose ten dollars seem a lot less prone to bargain over the price of a soda."

Longarm didn't want to head down that trail. He'd heard all the pros and cons at many a cow town council meeting, and had never heard a final solution to the paradox. It was simply a fact of human nature that combining hard liquor and high-stakes gambling with other forms of public entertainment sent profits through the roof and many a man, woman, or worse to an early grave.

He steered Rosemary on to other gossip she'd heard around the lot thanks to her naturally curious nature. Some of the married-up tent show folk were living as dangerously as you'd find in your average working-class neighborhood or country-club set, but nobody had been screwing around with automatons as far as Rosemary had heard. Longarm had assumed the few who'd viewed the body of Professor Lewis close up had either been discreet or assumed his poor old pecker had come out of his pants naturally as he struggled for his life.

She asked Longarm if he wanted more when she saw he'd polished off the last of his tin plate. She sounded a bit wistful when he said he aimed to scout about some more on horseback. So he asked if she wanted to tag along. But she didn't have her own mount up the line, and added, sort of pouty, "I was planning on turning in for a few hours of beauty rest. When you work such spotty hours after dark, you learn to grab such time in bed as your luck may allow."

He offered to help with the dishes before he rode out across the surrounding reed flats. But she told him to just ride on all he had to, and added, "I'd have never fed you all those onions if you'd told me you had other engagements for this afternoon."

So, as they rose, he hauled her in for a friendly kiss, which left her staring wide-eyed and breathless as he calmly told her, "You ate as many onions as me and I didn't notice 'em all that much just now."

Then he turned to duck out the tent flap, grinning as he strode back along that boxed-in power train laid out to the rear of the show tents facing the still-deserted midway.

He didn't hear any machinery running. He wondered idly why the late Professor Lewis had never thought to power his mechanical wonders by steam. He decided an automaton with an obvious steam line or drive shaft up the ass might look less wondrous. The notion that even a wizard could build an automaton that got around with no outside source of power for any length of time was just silly.

Back at the rope corral he found that young wrangler jawing with Luke Blair, the boss of the security clowns. Blair said he'd just ridden out from town, and that most of the others would be along by no later than three to get set up for the evening show.

Blair said they hadn't turned Ray Harmon loose yet, the stubborn Mormon mules, and so he doubted Miss Judith would be out to open the professor's particular show. Longarm said the wispy blonde had told him she didn't know too much about the wind-up toys her dear dad had left her, and added, "I just had a look-see around their show tent. Kid Clang never came home last night. But what do you think of these?"

Blair took the two brass shells Longarm offered and held them up to the light, saying, "Peterson blank and an army-issue .45-28. What about 'em? We know that clockwork killer fired blanks, when he was working right, and that asshole kid who shot him out of order did so with real bullets."

Longarm said soberly, "Lockport Krankheit favors a double-action .38, worn quick-draw in a tied-down buscadero rig. Ida Foyle was hit in the head with a .45. Another lady just pointed out that there was a Schofield .45 at the end of that automaton's waving right forearm."

Blair snorted, "Tell me something I never knew before. Did you think you were the only one scouting for sign last night? Me and my boys were the ones made to look bad by that murderous tick-tock. So, sure, we thought about that junky old Schofield. Then we thought some more about it being a single-action thumb-buster in a tin hand with no thumb."

Longarm said, "I noticed. Meanwhile, as many a gun-smith might know, converting single- to double-action involves no more than reworking the internal sears between trigger and hammer. If you want it easier, what's wrong with an extra push rod, pull wire, or some such simple wonder running out along that hinged forearm to cock a plain old single-action loaded six-in-the-wheel with .45-28s?"

Blair suggested, "Try it even easier. There's a peep-hole just above the spot where that quick-draw contest was held. Say somebody inside the tent had another gun of *any* description and a hard-on for *you*, standing as close as you were to that Mormon gal he got instead, by shooting without aiming right, through that canvas he was hiding behind!"

Longarm said that wouldn't work.

Blair demanded, "Why not? Ray was making his pitch out front. Judy Harmon had no call to look inside before their show began either. It would have been simple for the killer, I mean a flesh-and-blood killer, to slip in the back way and—"

"I've already peered through that peephole," Longarm cut in, taking back the shell casings. "There were even some other holes lower down I considered. But then we're stuck with the timing. How could anyone have known some sore loser was going to spin Kid Clang my way, or that I'd be there at all, as he went pussyfooting around the back way?"

Blair was trying out another notion involving a jealous Mormon husband or rejected lover by the time Longarm had saddled, bridled, and mounted his hired paint. As the wrangler opened the gate ropes for him, he suggested Blair have his clowns poke about the lot for some wound-down clockwork before someone could wind it up some more. Blair grumbled, "We looked high and low. I even asked the colonel and Mr. Cotter to let me search their locked wagons personally. That son-of-a-bitching Kid Clang just can't be on the lot no more. But I just don't him walking away on his own!"

Longarm agreed that made two of them, and rode out and off the fairgrounds, hoping Rosemary was wrong about that rain.

Burnt-over reed flats looked glum enough under sunny skies. As he rode across the blackened stubble, the hooves of his pony stirring stirrup-deep clouds of soot,

Longarm saw enough distant rooftops, in all directions, to account for the criss-cross tangle of narrow paths or rutted traces running every which way from the fairgrounds. He muttered to his mount, "We're on a pure foolish errand, Paint. If the son-of-a-bitching automaton strode bold as brass on his own tin boots across this stubble and drifting ash, a paid-up bloodhound, even a tin one, would never be able to cut his son-of-a-bitching trail out this way!"

But it was nice riding weather despite the overcast, and a man never knew how much he might need to know about the range he was riding across if he had to ride at night. So Longarm lit a cheroot and rode west toward the Great Salt Lake.

They never got there. They soon passed the last of the burn-off, and managed a mile or so into dead but still-standing reeds before the path he'd founded ended at a deserted duck blind with slimy mud and open patches of clear brine beyond. So Longarm turned back, observing, "Anyone we chase this way won't be a native from around here, Paint."

The pony, who was, didn't seem to care. Longarm doubted any of the local folks could be behind much of this shit. Nobody from Utah could have set that death trap for a dirty old man in Nebraska, and the twisted human mind behind all this clockwork skullduggery had to know a thing or two about the layout of the show, as well as a thing or *three* about clockwork.

He found another duck hunter's path trending south and followed it, aiming to make a wide circuit of the surrounding range in order to ride it better when and if he felt more pressed for time.

Like Salt Lake City itself, to the south, Odgen perforce lay back clean out of sight of open salty water. For aside from soggy building sites, the once far larger inland sea offered well water too salty for mules for a good eight or ten miles inland from its low, gently sloping shores.

Hence they circled far and wide indeed before Longarm was lured by sunflower windmills against the gray sky to a quarter-section spread growing table beets and lamb chops for the Union Pacific's dining cars.

The friendly old Saint who owned the spread was surrounded by a snow-white beard and a dozen gals ranging in age from, say, fifteen to fifty. Longarm didn't ask how many might be wives or daughters. He'd long since found he got along better with Mexicans and Mormons if he pretended their womenfolk weren't there. But he had to thank the sassy young redhead who handed him a glass of lemonade when he dismounted to sit a spell with the old Saint on the front steps.

Salty lemonade was all right, he decided, once he got over the surprise. They were doubtless more used to their well water. Folks who farmed the Mormon Delta were good at nursing themselves, their stock, and even crops on uncertain water supplies. Longarm knew you could grow beets and even barley with water that would pickle most truck or grain in the fields, provided you got enough rain now and again to sweeten your irrigation ditches a mite. Stock that lived on grass and grain got some *good* out of salt in their water, as long as it wasn't overdone.

A shipwrecked sailor or a traveler lost on the desert was better off drinking nothing than sipping saltwater that would make him pee more. But providing you put *other* liquids away, such as apple juice or tomato preserves, for your kidneys to cope with, you could take plenty of salt in your well water, and in the western reaches of the Mormon Delta, they did.

The old farmer and his collection of salt-swilling females had heard there was a tent show over to the fairgrounds, but hadn't gone and didn't expect to go, there being a limit to how many table beets a railroad would buy. So there was something to Rosemary's bitch about poor business in these remote parts of the West. He'd have liked to ask Joy Hayward about that, if she hadn't been dead.

He found himself wondering about that even as the old Saint went on about statehood for Deseret, as the older Saints insisted on calling Utah.

Being neither a Mormon nor a Ute, Longarm didn't really care to argue about that. The killer might have been out to do him in along with Joy, or either one of them alone could have been the intended target of a shotgun blast in tricky light. It was obvious why some crook might want a lawman with a rep for catching crooks to just die and let a poor crook get on with it. Trying to figure why someone would gun a gal who'd surely never meant to book her own show into places where they'd make no money got him nowhere. He politely turned down the offer of a second salty lemonade, lest he piss all the way back to the fairgrounds, and excused himself from a supper invitation as well to ride on.

A total circuit would have taken him back into Ogden. He knew what lay over that way. So he walked his pony in from the east, only dismounting to piss twice on the open dead-flat range, more grassy than reedy, off to the east.

By the time he had his paint back in that rope corral and his gear in the tack tent, he'd learned everyone but Judith Harmon had returned from town. Stakes Slade, when they ran into one another, told him Harmon's wife didn't mean to open their show at all till they let her Raymond out. Slade couldn't say whether she was scared of things that went bump in the dark, or simply not able to make all that clockwork perform the way her menfolk had. Just as Longarm thought they were parting friendly, Slade growled, "Heard you've been sort of sparking Cupcakes O'Dowd. Let me give you a friendly word of advice. Don't."

Longarm turned back to face him, smiling thinly as he soberly replied, "I didn't think I was. But now that you mention it, what were you planning on doing about it if I *did* help myself to a bit more popcorn, friend?"

Slade smiled right back. "Me? Nothing. I'm too young to die over anything replaceable as a woman. But maybe I ain't the only man in this show and . . . You do as you like, Rube. Just don't say you were never warned."

Then he spun on one heel and strode away, humming that familiar tune involving an honest young cowhand led astray by a false-hearted woman. Longarm figured he could ask old Rosemary if she was spoken for and by whom, if it ever started to matter that much.

Passing a big red shed on wheels, Longarm spied that paper-pusher and property master, Cotter, coming out with a big cigar in his mouth and a bemused expression on his face. As they met near the bottom of the steps Cotter nodded and said, "Blair told me you were on the lot. Still no word about that clockwork killer, I suppose?"

Longarm shook his head. "That's no reason to quit looking. Once I find it I might have a better grasp on who makes it tick. Blair says he's already searched your wagon there. What exactly is it, a safe place to keep tickets, cash receipts, and such?"

Cotter said, "Exactly. The Mosler combination safe I just put a bank withdrawal in makes a nice second line of defense. Would you like a look inside?"

Longarm asked, "Why? Do you have Kid Clang in there?"

Cotter laughed. "I was *with* Joy Hayward, not clanking *after* her, that night. But seriously, where do you think the real killer could have hidden that thing?"

Longarm shrugged. "Not out on the open range all about. I just rode over it some. Let me ask you something else. Was Joy Hayward following orders from you or Colonel Palmer when she picked Ogden as your next stop?"

Cotter answered easily. "I'm only responsible for managing the owners' cash and valuables. I have nothing to say about how they ought to go about *getting* it." Then, less surely, he went on. "I just don't know whether she handled advance bookings completely on her own or as directed by Colonel Palmer. You'll have to ask *him*. I admired poor Joy, a lot, but we were never as . . . close."

Longarm kept a poker face as he digested that unwelcome thought. Then he decided it was fair for a gal to get close with her boss since she hadn't yet met a randy cuss who got close with coffee shop gals. But he still found himself muttering, "Since we seem to be on that subject. Might you know how . . . close anyone else might feel toward, say, Judith Harmon, or maybe Rosemary O'Dowd?"

Cotter looked incredulous. "Miss Judith is a married woman as well as, well, let's face it, sort of flighty for such a plain little thing. As for Cupcakes? I don't think so. Poor Slade made quite a play for her, when first she joined our show. But she never showed any interest, and I don't think anyone else has an inside track with her. Why are we gossiping like this, Deputy Long?"

Longarm said, "It ain't gossip when it's a murder investigation. We got us this handbook written by a famous French detective, only printed in English. He says to consider the opportunity, means, and motive of every possible suspect and then, when in doubt, search for the pussy. I got more suspects with the means to have done something than I could shake a stick at. I'm still working on motive, cash or pussy having motivated more killers than I like to think about. Cash don't work as simple as pussy up to now. Everyone agrees this show's barely clearing enough profit to limp from town to town at the moment, and anybody out to crack that safe inside ought to have done so and lit out with the loot by now."

"I can show you we've less than a thousand on hand, counting the cash I just put in. We have to keep a certain amount on hand to make change and handle petty-cash emergencies."

Longarm replied, "I just said that. Two of the victims we're supposed to buy as machine-made murder victims were good-looking gals. I can't connect 'em in any other way. That murder made to look like a sort of industrial accident in Omaha had a pussy angle too, even though you'd be surprised whose pussy was involved."

Cotter shook his head soberly and softly said, "No I wouldn't. The colonel read the coroner's report as well. The poor old man must have been getting senile as well as sex-starved. The medical examiner back there told us a surprising number of lonely men, and women, manage to kill themselves with instruments never intended to be substituted for sex organs."

Longarm nodded wearily. "There was this old maid over to Denver, bled to death getting way too friendly with a baseball bat. She was using the small end, of

156

course, but it was still more than she was built to take that deep. The Denver coroner's office wrote her death up sort of gallantly to protect her memory, come to study on it. But that time there was no question of homicide in mind."

Cotter snorted, "Nor in the death of that silly old man, I'd wager. Assuming a total fiend out to murder a man with his own automaton, who on earth would expect a man in his sixties to be enjoying the favors of a clockwork ballerina after hours?"

Longarm said flatly, "Someone who peeked through holes in a front wall, with the midway dark, or felt up pretty but lifeless ladies often enough to discover one had a secret pussy? I'm not too clear on just how someone built some extra tricks into a sort of frisky clockwork dancing gal. But once they did, well, you know the awkward position he was found in."

Cotter grimaced and declared, "With his back broken. The Omaha coroner's office said he'd have never been able to breathe, held so tight, had that steel grab not snapped his poor spine!"

Longarm said, "Well, I don't have to search for *that* pussy. But I'd best mosey on in search of what could be a pussy-crazed killer."

Cotter said, "I don't see how a mechanical man could be after anything like that!"

Longarm replied, "That's what I just said," as he went off to see what Rosemary O'Dowd had to say about men fighting over her or any other gals with the show.

# Chapter 11

There was much to be said for painted canvas when you were a lawman innocently moving in the back way to hear somebody mad as a wet hen giving somebody else holy hell.

Longarm had no trouble recognizing the angry voice of Rosemary O'Dowd. The spunky little gal was inclined to talk pungently even when feeling friendly. As he moved around to eavesdrop in a slot between Rosemary's red tent and the green one next door, he realized the male voice trying to calm Rosemary down belonged to old Colonel Palmer. He figured he was more likely to learn what the fuss was about faster if he just listened.

He was right. Rosemary declared, "You horny old shit, there ain't enough money to buy this child's ass for the likes of you!"

To which the old man soothingly replied, "You're taking this all wrong, Miss Rosemary. I never said anything about asking for bedroom privileges if you'd rather work more directly under me!"

Rosemary snorted, "I never said I wanted to work anywhere on this lot. I said I was leaving. Have you got wax in your ears?"

Colonel Palmer replied, "And *I* said you could take Miss Joy Hayward's place as my advance agent if you're not satisfied with your refreshment concession."

Rosemary sounded just as insistent as she retorted, "There's nothing wrong with my popcorn, and I'm changing to another brand of orange soda. I've always done plenty of business, even with a shitty brand of soda, when there was any business to be done."

He said, "Now, Miss Rosemary, you know I tried to move on to Elko, clean out of this Mormon country, as soon as we saw how slow things were here in Ogden. Is it my fault the authorities won't let me budge that train while they're still holding Raymond Harmon as some sort of mechanical monster?"

She said, "It's your fault you picked a cow town in Nevada, so long after the fall roundup, as your next stop! Don't you know anything about your own business, Colonel? Winter will soon be upon us, and you expect me to sell popcorn and soda in the high desert of Nevada? To who? Digger Indians? If you'd had the brains to hire an advance agent who knew the business, instead of how to please a dirty old man, we'd be touring the Old South right now, where the tents stay easy to heat and the rubes are better sports, as well as more numerous!"

The colonel blustered, "Who ever told you there was anything at all dirty going on between me and poor Joy Hayward?"

Longarm wanted to know too. So he listened sharp as Rosemary said, "Never mind who told me. Suffice it to say, you don't know all the knotholes in that big office wagon you hold court in, and like I said, I'd never in this world go down on a man too old to get it up right!"

Having kissed Joy a lot, Longarm could only hope Colonel Palmer was being truthful as he loudly declared, "Now that, young lady, is a monstrous lie! To begin with, I can still get it up as need be, as my own dear wife back East would be the first to tell you, after she'd snatched you bald-headed!"

Rosemary sniffed and replied, "Well, I'll allow the Peeping Tom who told me has a dirty mouth about *all* us gals, if *you'll* allow a gal with so little common sense about bookings certainly must have had *some* hold on you. I'm not the only one who's been saying this tour has been a disaster since that last good gate back in Omaha."

Palmer sighed and said, "All right, I'll admit my late partner, Lewis, had perhaps a better grasp of geography than Miss Joy or me. But I was the one who knew how to pack up, move on, and set up this show. As to whether I know where I'm going or not, you just heard me offer you the chance to pick our next site once they let poor Harmon out!"

Rosemary sounded somewhat mollified as she cautiously replied, "Virginia City is only another few hours by rail and one hell of a lot more populated, by hardrock miners, than Elko. After that I'd get us the hell over the Sierras, and follow the warm weather down the California settlements to swing back towards real tent-show country by way of Texas, New Orleans, and such. So how come we have to wait on the Harmons? Can't they catch up, once that nice Deputy Long proves Ray innocent by catching the real killer?"

Colonel Palmer said, "I wish things were that simple. I just told you they've forbidden any of us to leave Ogden Township. I fear that includes you. So how do you think that federal man is coming with the killing of poor Joy and that Mormon girl?"

Rosemary sighed and said, "I don't know. I wish he'd either catch the rascal so's I could move on, or act more like a rascal around a poor traveling gal who's just plain bored to death out here in the middle of nowhere!"

Colonel Palmer dryly asked, "Would you take Joy Hayward's job if I gave my blessings to your romance with that good-looking young lawman?"

She laughed self-mockingly and said, "He doesn't know we're having a romance, and I wouldn't have poor Joy's job even if I thought you knew this business."

Longarm wasn't surprised to hear Colonel Palmer bluster he'd been touring with tent shows before she was born. But Rosemary had no respect for her elders, or else felt older than she looked. For she simply told him, "You may be a sweet old asshole, Colonel. But an asshole is an asshole. You just can't make money with a tent show that offers no real excitement. Folks don't load up the buggy and go clean out of town to study a few freaks, play penny a pitch, or even buy my swell popcorn. You got to offer them something a heap more exciting than what they can see anytime in their own hick world."

Longarm felt sort of sorry for the old man as Palmer pleaded, "Dang it, Miss Rosemary, you know how I feel about hard liquor, high-stakes gambling, and other improper entertainments!"

She demurely replied, "Of course I do. Didn't you just hear me say I want to get out of here? Trying to run a prim and proper tent show is like trying to run a prim and proper whorehouse, Colonel. Prim and proper folks don't go to either, unless they feel way less prim and proper than they may let on. Rubes riding out to bright lights and quick-time organ music *expect* to see shocking sights and a chance to double their hick pocket jingle or lose it all! I mind when my man, Frank, and me were set up next to this tattooed lady, who was tattooed dirty in places only sports with an extra quarter were allowed to view in the back. Colonel, we sold more popcorn and cold beer that summer than I could pop or Frank could ice! And she never screwed a rube for money neither. She only shocked some loose change out of the silly things."

Colonel Palmer said stubbornly, "I've had this same discussion with others, Miss Rosemary. I meant what I said about allowing you or anyone else with the show to suggest better locations. But as long as I am running this show, I mean to run it as a decent show!"

The colonel must have figured that ended the discussion. For Longarm got the impression the gal was alone after he'd heard nothing but soft rustles in there for a spell. So he went around to the side with the flap, cleared his throat, and ducked inside.

Then he said, "Oops, sorry, there was nothing to knock on," as Rosemary hastily covered her naked charms down the front with the fancier concession stand smock she'd been changing into. Before she did he'd discovered she wore no underwear, and that those cupcakes were not only real but mighty spicy-looking.

He started to duck back out. She snapped, "Stay put. The damage is done, and isn't it a good thing we're country?"

He wasn't sure he knew exactly what she meant. So he looked away, and went through the pretense of groping for a smoke as she turned her bare back to him and slipped the smock on with a skill hinting at a history of living in mixed company at close quarters.

As she turned back to him, cupcakes covered and pinning up her wavy hair, she dimpled and said, "There, that wasn't so bad, was it? You just missed my telling Colonel Palmer off, the old fool."

Longarm said, "No, I didn't. I was right outside, listening in. It's surprising what a lawman picks up that way at times. Do you think Joy Hayward was really the old man's play-pretty before she was murdered by person or persons unknown?"

Rosemary went sort of pink as she replied, "You heard me repeat what I'd heard about them. Did you hear us, ah, talking about you and me?"

Longarm said soberly, "I did. I want you to study on my words before you bluster. One man with this show just told me to stay away from you. Another man just told me that same sport made a play for you and got turned down."

"You're talking about Stakes Slade," she said. "To answer your unspoken question, I'd screw Colonel Palmer before I'd even kiss *that* asshole, and you just heard me tell Colonel Palmer what I thought of screwing *him*!"

Longarm chuckled fondly, and said he admired a gal who knew her own mind. She said, "It's fixing to rain. I might open my concession after sundown. Then again, I might not. Meanwhile, that way bigger Lewis layout across the midway will be shut for certain until Lord knows when. So why don't we go back over there and, ah, hunt for more sign?"

He started to ask what she expected him to find over yonder now that he'd searched by night and by day. Then he wondered why any man would want to ask a dumb question like that. So they went over to fool with the exhibits, and one another, until, sure enough, it started to rain on the canvas above them and Rosemary said, "That tears it. I'm not about to get my popper all greasy again for any rainy-night gate. Did you notice that sofa they keep in one of the back rooms tacked on to this main tent?"

He said he had, next door to the workshop. Rosemary said it was where Judith Harmon stretched out between shows when she was suffering her female complaints. When Rosemary demurely added she'd just gotten over her own, he knew she was telling him flat out she didn't expect him to take any vulcanized precautions. So once they were seated back there on the overstuffed leather sofa, he swapped enough spit with her to keep her from thinking she was being raped, and then since she'd been so open about it, and since she wasn't wearing anything under her thin concession smock, they got down to what Colonel Palmer had already given his blessings to.

She allowed she admired *his* body too, once he'd shucked his own duds to mount her right as the rain pattered down on thick canvas above them. She wrapped her small strong legs around him, closed her eyes, and sobbed, "Oh, it's been so long since it's been this good!" He sensed what she really needed, more than the adventure itself. So they took their time and made it last, just moving enough to stay aroused, the way a married couple who really like one another might behave as overnight guests in the home of a maiden aunt they didn't want to keep awake. He knew he was treating her right when she suddenly sobbed, "Faster, Frank, I'm starting to come and, oh, my God, I'm sorry, Custis!"

He said soothingly, "Let it go. I understand, and ain't it just as well we're country?"

So she came, a long shuddering time, and he did too, as she laughed like hell, reminding him of somebody he'd never ever do that with again, bless both their sweet

164

bottoms. Then, since it felt so swell the first time, they did it some more, and a long rainy afternoon passed all too swiftly by as they spent the rest of it screwing, smoking, and talking.

By the time the rain and their first excitement seemed to be letting up, Longarm had naturally brought Rosemary up to date on his hunt for the clockwork killer, leaving out some parts that might have made her jealous. She was only able to clarify things he'd already figured pretty tight. But she found some of what he told her downright unbelievable. She said she'd never buy that notion about a rubber-pussied death trap until she saw it. Since by this time that steam organ was playing "Camptown Races" outside, he said they'd best get dressed and that then he'd show her how the poor old professor had managed to leave real young gals alone.

He took longer to dress than she did. So she was already out in the main tent, a lamp burning and that ballerina already doing her innocent dance, by the time he joined her, fastening the buckle of his gun rig.

Rosemary said, "Pooh, she isn't bumping and grinding like you said."

He nodded and warned, "Don't go groping at her underdrawers. I ain't sure whether the trigger under her rubber-belly hide is only released from inside her or not. For all we really know, old Lewis only shoved his gut against her too hard."

Rosemary let go of the hem of the dancing doll's dress, and moved back wide-eyed as Longarm moved around closer to the wall of the tent and hunkered down to swap cylinders, waiting until the pretty ballerina had taken her bow and stopped to see if they wanted an encore before he shoved that other brass, which only looked different on closer examination, under her bank of push rods.

Rosemary gasped, "Jesus H. Christ!" when Longarm got the sweet-looking ballerina to dancing more dirty. As the pretty automaton commenced to bump and grind with her elbows above her ears, Rosemary pouted, "That's not fair. Real gals aren't built so forward. But I guess I could move like that if that's the way you men like it, provided you could get it in me in that position."

Longarm chuckled and replied, "I ain't sure I could even get it up right now, thanks to your earlier efforts to please. I've told you why I'd never in this world want to stick it in *her!*"

"Put something up her and let me see her snap," Rosemary demanded.

Longarm gazed about, saying, "I forget where I left that crank. But maybe if I stand safely behind her and give her tummy a pat I could . . . That's something I hadn't considered before, and once a killer or killers changed cylinders, or just the duds and wigs . . ."

Longarm suddenly snapped his fingers and said, "Aw, hell, none are so blind as those who just won't see! I got to go make a heap of arrests now, honey. Where will you be, say, half an hour from now?"

She asked, "What's wrong with right here? Neither Judith nor Ray Harmon will be back from town tonight and everyone on the lot knows that. Who are you out to arrest, darling?"

But he was already on his way out the dripping front flap, to stalk up the lamp-lit but not so busy midway as the sun set somewhere in a soggy sky of rusty red.

Rosemary had been right about a lackluster show drawing a piss-poor gate from a town the size of Ogden. In the tricky light he saw nearly as many clown-suited security men and uniformed copper badges from town as there were paying visitors. The soggy afternoon, just as Rosemary had expected, had discouraged all but a few of the more adventurous young folks from riding out across the muddy flats, and those who'd come looked mostly country and hence under-funded for a tent show that was already operating well in the red.

A police sergeant he'd talked to in town fell in beside Longarm as, up ahead, that big merry-go-round was slowly turning with not a soul aboard any of the painted ponies as they bobbed far more tamely than the mounts most of the rubes had ridden out on.

The sergeant said he and his men had been sent out to make sure there was no more bullshit with clockwork killers, and added, "That Luke Blair in charge of security tells us his own boys have searched every nook and cranny out here without finding a sign of that wind-up Kid Clang."

Longarm said, "He told me the same thing. I'm way more intent on finding the son of a bitch who wound it up! That automaton was only what stage magicians call misdirection, designed to make us all look the wrong way while the slicker pulls something else out of another sleeve. Stick around. I see Colonel Palmer up by yonder merry-go-round, and he's somebody I want some answers out of!"

So the police sergeant tagged along as Longarm bore down on the older man and a clown-suited crowd handler. They were talking about the miserly crowd apparently, as Longarm caught the last few words of their unhappy conversation.

As the colonel saw Longarm and the gilt badge coming he smiled sort of wistfully and said, "Evening. I don't suppose I could get either of you to ride our

167

merry-go-round at a nickel a head?"

Longarm said, "Maybe another time, Colonel. Am I correct in assuming Miss Judith Harmon née Lewis is half owner of this whole shebang?"

Palmer smiled uncertainly and replied, "Close enough. She and her husband, of course, own forty percent. I hold the controlling interest of forty-one percent. Why do you ask?"

Longarm said thoughtfully, "Makes sense for her not to care about opening down the midway tonight, with her man in jail and them drawing the same profits from a show being run in the red, no offense."

Palmer blustered, "See here, I've done my best to show a profit, and if you know how to make a profit on rubes that don't know the name of their own territory, I wish you'd let me in on it!"

Longarm said, "Running this tent show ain't my beeswax exactly. But those figures you just cited are sort of interesting, Colonel. If you hold forty-one percent of the shares and the heirs of your late junior partner hold forty, that leaves nineteen percent, and so who might we be talking about?"

The old showman shrugged and said, "Quarter-share certificates are held by the owners of our more imposing pitches. You'd have to ask Mr. Cotter exactly who holds what. He keeps the books. Would you mind telling us what you're getting at, Deputy Long?"

Longarm would have, but just then a dunken snarl behind him said he was a yellow-livered son of a bitch, so Longarm spun round just in time to spy Lockport Krankheit just his side of the merry-go-round, red-faced with rage and gun hand hovering out to one side of his low-slung six-gun, as he announced, "I want everyone but Longarm to get the hell out of my line of fire so's we can have it out fair and square!"

Longarm said soothingly, "You got things wrong, Lockport. We don't have any sensible quarrel!"

Then he added, "Holy shit! Behind you, Lockport!" as he saw an even wilder-looking figure swinging into view aboard that merry-go-round.

Lockport sneered, "That trick's old as the hills, and now you are going to get it!" as he crabbed sideways, going for his sidearm as he did. So Longarm crabbed the other way, hoping against hope his cross-draw was at least as fast as a side-draw that had already started.

He never found out. For up on the turning platform behind the mean drunk, the steel hat shading his painted face, Kid Clang rode ramrod stiff on his firmly planted metal boot heels as he raised his own six-gun and fired, just as both Lockport and Longarm were zigging where less-experienced gunfighters might have zagged.

The .45 slug meant for Longarm hit Lockport in the back of his skull, to pop out his tongue and both eyeballs as his hat rose high on a geyser of gore. So Longarm pegged his own first shot at the impossible Kid Clang as the spin of the merry-go-round whipped him around out of sight again!

Behind Longarm, that police sergeant was shrilling his tin whistle. Longarm yelled, "Get that crowd out of pistol range. And that was a .45-60 wildcat if I'm any judge of such matters!"

Not wanting to stop a high-powered pistol round with his own head, Longarm passed the sprawled form of Lockport to circle the lit-up merry-go-round the way a steel-hatted killer had been coming, rather than going. In the tricky light beyond he thought he saw movement up by that stationary steam power plant. But then he heard pistol shots off in another direction and ran that way.

169

So did others. That police sergeant caught up with them as the even more confused-looking property master, Cotter, waved his own gun at the darkness beyond his office on wheels and shouted, "It went that way, on a damn clockwork pony! I don't know if I hit it or not. I know I can't believe what I just saw with my own eyes!"

Longarm said, "Neither can I. Drop that gun. I ain't going to say that twice, Cotter!"

Cotter didn't drop the Remington .41 he was gripping in his doubtless sweaty palm. Before he could do anything else with it, Longarm fired, aiming for the bastard's guts. He didn't do that because of Joy Hayward, or even the innocent Ida Foyle. As Cotter fell writhing at their feet Longarm told the sergeant, "Take down his dying statement. Have your men arrest everybody in a clown suit, gentle or firm as they have to. We'll separate the sheep from the goats when I get back to you!"

Then he was gone, as the sergeant wailed after him, "Where are you going, Longarm? This gut-shot cuss said the automaton headed out across the reed flats!"

That was too dumb to answer, even if Longarm had wanted anyone to know his own position as he circled behind the tents to the west of the midway.

He cursed himself silently for leaving Rosemary alone in that shut-down show tent everyone with the show would *expect* to be the best hideout on the lot. He had to shout, "Rosemary! Hit the dirt!" as he tore in through a rear flap. So somebody pegged a wild shot his way in the dark as he took his own advice and landed on one shoulder to roll behind the cast-iron base of some damned something.

An automaton swayed above him in the blackness. Longarm's invisible enemy fired at the slight disturbance. Longarm knew the son of a bitch would never hunker near that muzzle flash long enough to matter. But he had another idea. He groped with his free hand to find the switch, and set the creation above him tick-tocking and doing Lord only knows what in the dark. Miss Judith had said such odd goings-on sounded spooky.

The unseen other fired again, bouncing a wildcat slug off steel hide as Longarm slithered along behind other exhibits, setting each in motion as he passed, until it was even distracting to *him* in an ink-black arena. So he held his own fire, trying to make out more natural-sounding movements in the darkness until, somewhere outside, he heard Rosemary yelling, "Custis? Is that you making all that racket in there?"

He had to yell, "It is, and I ain't alone! Stay back and get help!" as his invisible enemy blasted three double-action shots at the sound of his voice.

Longarm had spoken from behind an iron Indian with that in mind, and firing more than once from the same stand had been the mistake Longarm had been hoping for. He fired once, and rolled a few yards along that end of the tent as he heard staggering footsteps, a muffled moan, and then a ghastly scream right after an ominous dull crunch.

Longarm had already guessed who it might be. So he recognized Luke Blair's weak voice as it pleaded, "Help me! It's squeezing me like a tube of oil paint and I'm shot in the breast besides!"

Longarm didn't answer. He'd tricked others in the dark that way in his own time. Then Rosemary O'Dowd tore in through the flap with a brightly burning lantern. She and the two copper badges with her could have got their fool heads blown off if old Luke Blair had not been so dead-looking yonder, held like a limp rag dolly in the steel arms of that dirty-dancing automaton, who'd knocked off her bumps and grinds to grab him good when Luke had stumbled into her in the dark with his less fatal injury.

The local lawmen were good sports about an outside lawman shooting it out with somebody local as soon as they spied the big horse pistol in the dust between Longarm and the still-oozing dead man. One of them picked it up, sniffed, and said, "Fired a heap, with that odd-smelling and hard-kicking gun cotton. Must have been out to kill somebody serious!"

Longarm said, "I suspect it was Colonel Palmer, in front of a crowd that might testify it was another industrial accident. Blair just happened on me and poor old Lockport Krankheit. Must have reloaded somewhere along the way. So the wildcat rounds in his gunbelt ought to prove Kid Clang was really Luke Blair."

Rosemary demanded, "Then where's the real automaton?"

So Longarm pointed with his own reloaded gun towards the back as he replied, "Where he's been all the time, of course. Stretched out in plain view atop a workbench with a few external as well as hasty alterations. That clockwork pony was doubtless taken apart and scattered about earlier. But there ought to be an extra tin head around here somewhere."

There was. One of the copper badges had just found the steel-brimmed hat and masklike face of the so-called Kid Clang, under a wind-up fortune-teller in a far corner, when that police sergeant tore in with Colonel Palmer to demand some damned explanations.

The sergeant said, "That property master you gut-shot doubtless died a lot later than he wanted to, but too sudden for us to get a whole lot of sense out of. He blames you for all the blood and slaughter around here,

172

and says it never would have happened if somebody had done something about your joy. Does that make any sense to you?"

Longarm smiled uncertainly, and pointed at the dead man hanging limply in the tender-looking embrace of the pretty ballerina. "That dead skunk likely shotgunned Joy Hayward after he'd been told by one of his paid sneaks I'd escorted her back to that parked railroad car. I'm still working on whether they gunned a female confederate thinking they were gunning me, or whether they were confounded by her taking so long to kill me *her* way and suspected she might be switching sides."

Rosemary marveled, "Oh, then I was right about you and that Joy Hayward fooling around behind the colonel's back!"

Colonel Palmer said, "Damn it! That dear child was never more than my advance agent to me! It was Cotter she was sweet on, if we have to speak ill of the dead."

Rosemary had accused Longarm of being her dead husband while she was coming with him. So he figured it was only fair to explain, "She and Cotter both lied to me about mechanical men clinking and clanking after them in the hopes of getting me to a more remote execution site. That part worked. But I passed on the chance to doze off in her tender arms so she could pull a Samson and Delilah on me."

Rosemary pouted, "Oh, Custis, how could you?"

To which he could only reply, "She was taking advantage of my weak nature. She spotted me on a train, when I wasn't even aware of this tent show, and leaped to the wrong conclusions. She must have known my rep, and she and her fellow plotters had doubtless talked about the federal angles once they'd left a murder victim buried on the far side of a state line."

Colonel Palmer pleaded, "Can't we get to what in blue blazes they were plotting? You've convinced me they killed my old pard and that I should have been paying closer attention to at least three people I thought I could trust, but what could they have been after, damn it?"

Longarm said, "Your show, to run it their way, more profitably. Joy Hayward was booking you dumb deliberately, in hopes of making an already tame show do even worse, no offense. Meanwhile, I've no doubt Cotter, acting generous and understanding, was buying up a quarter-share here and a half-share there."

Rosemary brightened and volunteered, "He gave me a hundred bucks for my quarter-share back in Wyoming, when first I mentioned I'd as soon leave such a tedious tour. I hadn't collected any dividends this side of the Mississippi and I needed the money."

Colonel Palmer paled and said, "Good Lord, what a two-faced son of a bitch! But even saying Cotter had managed to buy a full nineteen percent of the show, the Harmons and I, between us—"

"Would have had eighty-one percent," Longarm finished. "Their forty and Cotter's nineteen would have had you outvoted and they wouldn't have needed to kill you. But maybe some of the other junior partners were more stubborn than Miss Rosemary here. Or maybe they'd just gotten in the habit, and felt no call to share any profits with you after they'd demoted you to junior partner. I aimed low at Cotter in hopes he'd clear such loose ends up."

The police sergeant marveled, "So you did, right after he lied to us about the way his confederate yonder had lit out. How come you were so sure he was lying, Longarm? I confess I only found it astounding, after seeing what seemed a clockwork killer killing with my own eyes!"

Longarm smiled modestly. "Oh, an automaton mounted on a clockwork pony was barely possible. But I'd caught him in a lie for certain earlier."

Pointing at the ballerina, still holding Luke Blair in her deadly dainty-looking arms, Longarm explained, "We call it guilty knowledge in the trade. The slicker who set that ballet dancer to surprise gents like that hadn't wanted her examined right, lest a machinist, say, half as good declared her a deliberate death trap. So after she snapped on Professor Lewis, they swapped her brass music-box drum with that harmless Viking princess, along with both wigs and costumes."

He turned to Colonel Palmer. "You were there that grim morning, Colonel. Tell us what you saw."

The old showman stared at the limp form of Luke Blair as he remembered. "Lewis was facing the other way, with his back broken and, well, sorry, Miss Rosemary, his pants down. But it was that other one, the Viking gal, or at least I think it was. You have me confused now."

Longarm nodded. "You and everyone who wasn't in on it were supposed to be confused. Is it safe to assume nobody saw fit to examine that other automaton, dressed like a ballerina, as you all pried Lewis loose from what seemed to be the Viking gal and doubtless found how ingeniously she'd been made under her chain mail?"

Colonel Palmer looked away from Rosemary as he murmured, "We felt we had to hush that part up. We did have a machinist back in Omaha examine the poor old fool's love toy. He said as far as he could tell the internal clockwork didn't do anything. He said he suspected she was a failed experiment. His analogy was that of a cuckoo clock that might hit you in the eye with loose parts instead of telling you what time it was. He

175

said he had no idea why her arms had clamped around the poor man like that."

Longarm nodded. "That left the death an open question, instead of a homicide for certain, which would have meant a tighter investigation all around. Being property master, and having the head of security on tap, it would have been simple for Cotter to switch costumes, wigs, and parts around to where nobody checking that Viking gal, like I did, could ever put together a clearer picture. I had me a time putting things together after I *did* see which clockwork gal was a killer."

Colonel Palmer said, "I see it all now. Not daring to get rid of the evidence for good, as long as it seemed the property of my dead pard's heirs, they framed poor Ray Harmon to get him out of the way, and if you hadn't exposed them tonight, with both Ray and Miss Judith in town—"

"You really do need someone to lead you around on a leash, no offense," Longarm said. He pointed to Rosemary with his chin as he suggested, "I'll bet Miss Rosemary *would* make a better advance agent than Cotter's play-pretty, if you pay her enough and treat her decent, like you offered before."

The police sergeant horned in to say, "The colonel don't sound so dumb to me. You've got me sold on yonder clockwork gal being designed to kill folks, and the one she just killed had killed both Ida Foyle and that Joy Hayward gal!"

Longarm said, "I wish you gents wouldn't finish my own fool sentences for me. Eating this apple a bite at a time, Cotter casually allowed to me that Professor Lewis had been done in by his ballet-dancing automaton. But anyone who hadn't been in on the plot would have been confused as everyone else as to *which* mechanical lady

176

had mousetrapped a dirty old man."

Everyone there but Longarm gaped in dawning understanding. He said, "I figured Luke Blair for a liar when he said he'd searched Cotter's office wagon for Kid Clang. That wasn't to keep me from poking about in there. It was to inspire me to think about that and other such places a clockwork killer might get to on its own. A stage-magic gal I used to know called that misdirection."

Rosemary asked what else that other gal had taught him, so he said, "Shell game and three-card monte works the same way. Get the sucker thinking about dumb places to look, and he might overlook a stripped-down automaton lying on a workbench in plain sight."

The police sergeant said, "That dying Cotter cuss said you were so smart they should have drowned you at birth. We'll get the rest out of those security clowns and roustabouts outside."

Longarm blinked and asked, "You arrested all of 'em, including old Stakes Slade and his crew?"

The local lawman said, "You told us to. I know most of 'em are innocent. I got ears. But some of 'em must have been in on it, and I don't see how we're ever going to get Cotter, his gal, or yonder killers, mechanical or otherwise, to tell us much."

Longarm said, "I doubt Slade had the brains to be let in on it. But letting him sweat may cure his natural trouble-making. Meanwhile, what say we go into town and see what the Harmons can tell us about all this?"

Colonel Palmer said, "By gum, that's right! I'd forgotten all about poor Raymond Harmon being framed for the killing of that Mormon girl and the wounding of so many others. It was that skunk Luke just pretending to be an automaton all the time, right?"

Longarm smiled down at Rosemary and murmured, "He and the others really need you, honey. Tell him again about your planned tour down the West Coast and back to civilization by way of warmer climes."

She said not to rush her. So Longarm suggested they all get on into town. But that police sergeant said, "I dunno, Longarm. I follow your drift, but it's getting late in the evening to let a man out when they're holding him on a homicide charge!"

Longarm sighed and asked, "Didn't you just hear the lady say not to rush her? That goes for me too. I swear I have never met so many folks anxious to jump the gun in one bunch."

Then, as he led the way out, he added, "I reckon that's what they were figuring on. It's small wonder they were out to kill me too long before I knew I was on the case."

178

# Chapter 12

By the time they got themselves, those dead bodies, and all their prisoners into town, it was even later. But Judith Harmon had somehow heard they were coming, and met them out front of the jail. When Colonel Palmer started to explain how they'd just found out Luke Blair had been Kid Clang all the time, Longarm suggested Rosemary and the colonel wait over at the Union Hotel while he and the other lawmen cleared up some details with her man.

Meanwhile, the sergeant had scouted up his watch commander and some other local officials. So they had to take Ray Harmon out of his tiny cell and question him in the wardroom, with a stenographer of the male persuasion taking notes.

Harmon seemed surprised, but hardly displeased, to hear a cuss dressed up like one of his automatons had been hugged to death by the same love toy that had killed his late father-in-law. He said he meant to get rid of such a dangerous exhibit once they turned him loose.

Longarm said, "We got a few details to clear up first. We know who the ringleaders were. We still have to sort out those few watchmen and roustabouts it would

179

have taken to do the heavy work. For some reason all the old boys we have in the jail at the moment seem just as convincing in their protestations of innocence."

Harmon smiled wanly and said, "I know just how they feel. How the *innocent* ones feel, at any rate. I was in the original line of fire when—Luke, you say—took the place of my quick-draw tin man?"

Longarm said, "Aw, come on, I was there too. We both know it was the automaton that swung around on one foot to shoot up the crowd when that fool cowhand jarred it out of commission with his own wild shooting. For Pete's sake, I shot it myself and watched its silk shirt burn half off. Who moved it inside later?"

Harmon asked, "How should I know? You were there when I was arrested on the spot. I told you before I had no idea how they could have got it to behave so wild. But ain't it obvious that if that fool kid hadn't spun it half around like that, it would have been aiming right at *me* instead of that poor Mormon gal when it started shooting real bullets some fool way?"

Longarm smiled thinly and declared, "There was nothing all that tricky about the way Kid Clang commenced shooting live rounds out that same repeating-rifle action, once it used up the first batch of blanks."

Harmon said, "I told you about the spacing of that hopper, damn it. It must have been the old gun I thought was empty. Right?"

Longarm said, "It *was* empty. I noticed you cocking it. Nice touch. As for the hopper being all wrong for live rounds, it's been my experience that, given an even-money bet between complicated and simple, it's smarter to go with simple. A man could say anything he wanted about the innards of a clockwork killer that wasn't there. But you see, we found Kid Clang, with a clown's head

180

on, flat on his tin ass in the back, not fifty feet from where he shot up a heap of innocent folk with live rounds from the same damn source!"

Harmon shrugged. "I suppose it would have been possible for Luke Blair to rework my original design a mite. Who's to say what a man pretending to be a tin man might do with some tin snips? That still leaves me the intended victim that night, don't it?"

Longarm could see he'd scored a point with some of the other lawmen crowded all about. He just nodded. "I considered that a lot when Miss Rosemary and me first pictured just where everyone would have been standing or sitting at the moment Kid Clang went *loco en la cabeza* that night. We could see the holes in the platform where the automaton's feet were supposed to be planted. But I kept my natural suspicions about your wife to myself, of course, till I'd taken time to mull 'em over good."

A police captain demanded, "Jesus H. Christ, you think Judith Harmon was in with those other rats?"

Longarm replied, "I said I'd considered it. Nasty things happen in the best of families. A lot of young gals can really work up a grudge against a doting daddy who dotes too much on 'em, and even a sincerely loving little thing might not always be a dirty old man's real daughter."

He reached absently for a smoke, remembered where he was, and forgot it, saying, "I put such dirty notions together with the way it seemed Ray here was the intended target. Then I pictured even the dirtiest old man sneaking some sort of pathetic slap-and-tickle with a machine when he had even an ugly old *real* gal to screw. I know you gents might find this hard to swallow, but even a fat and silly gal is way more tempting than a sort of glorified hot-water bottle."

He got no argument about that. So he continued. "If Miss Judith was really the professor's lawful heiress, that would be all the more reason for one of the plotters aiming to take over the show to marry up with her, courting insistently, right after they got rid of the colonel's junior partner."

Harmon said, "I don't like what you seem to be getting at! I was courting Judy before her dad had that accident, and such shares in the show as she inherited are still in her name!"

Longarm nodded. "That's doubtless why you were checked into a hotel with another woman the night they sprung the trap on her father. Was it you and Joy Hayward, just to set up an alibi, or did you just trust to luck and scout up some town gal in a hotel taproom?"

Harmon half wailed, "A man has feelings, and Judy insisted we wait until our wedding night! Never mind about me and old Joy. You still can't get around the simple fact that it would have been *me,* nobody else, that malfunctioning automaton would have killed if it hadn't been for that mean drunk! Are you trying to say he was in this crazy overcomplicated plot you've come up with?"

Longarm said, "Not hardly. Lockport's wild shooting complicated what had started out more simple. I just mentioned those holes drilled in the platform to hold your automaton's feet. Both feet. But had both feet been positioned right, smacking Kid Clang's iron hide with soft lead never would have spun him around like so. I put it to you that you'd taken a heel pin out, to shift your quick-draw exhibit just a mite. Just a mite would have done it, with your wife sitting there like a pretty little hen, with her head at the same level as that quick-draw artist's belly-gun!"

Harmon turned to the senior officer in the room to wave Longarm off and demand, "Do I have to listen to any more of this maniac's fairy tales, Captain? There's no way I can prove such wild notions wrong. I can't prove there ain't a big pink elephant up on the roof. It's up to the one who says it's there to prove it's there. We all know the burden of proof ain't on the accused, right?"

The captain smiled uncertainly at Longarm and asked, "Could you show us that pink elephant on the roof, Deputy Long?"

Longarm said, "Don't have to. Got this asshole in the box with testimony from a smarter sidekick. Only wanted to tidy up some of the loose ends and figured he could use a break."

Turning back to Harmon, he said sweetly, "Could you use a break, asshole?"

Harmon naturally, although cautiously, wanted to know just what Longarm had in mind.

Longarm said, "That's better. Listen tight. As I understand the criminal code of Utah Territory, a condemned murderer gets the choice of death by hanging or by firing squad."

Harmon muttered, "That's some choice, and I never murdered anyone, damn your eyes!"

Longarm said, "Somebody did. A Utah court is surely going to execute at least one of you for the killing of their own Miss Ida Foyle. On the other hand, justice will only demand one life for her untimely death. They'll likely settle for Luke Blair as the killer of Joy Hayward and Lockport Krankheit. That leaves us with you and your pal, Cotter, who says *you* were the mastermind behind all this skullduggery."

Harmon sobbed, "That's a fucking lie! *He* was the one who came up with the whole scheme in the beginning!

183

None of the rest of us knew anything about business shares! I joined the show fair and square back East. I never would have even looked at that flat-chested Judy had not Cotter and that two-faced Joy Hayward got me to one side and showed me how we could all get rich."

Longarm didn't want to know exactly what Joy might have done to convince the treacherous son of a bitch. At least Longarm could say he'd never been down on the bitch, now that he saw how much hurt he'd wasted on a two-faced Delilah.

Once Longarm had cracked Harmon's wall of silence, it burst like a dam to spill the self-serving bile of an ambitious small-town shit. When Longarm had heard enough to prove he'd guessed about right on the basics, he stepped out in the corridor to see if his last cheroot would cut the sour taste in his mouth.

It didn't help much. But he was still smoking it when the same sergeant from out at the fairgrounds came out to join him. The somewhat older Saint politely ignored the sin gripped by Longarm's teeth as he said, "He's sure singing songs and naming names for us in there now, thanks to your little white lie about a mastermind who didn't want to be half as helpful. But was tricking Harmon that way constitutional, Deputy Long?"

Longarm blew smoke out both nostrils, but showed no obvious rage in his voice as he declared, "It ought to be, till the Supreme Court says we ain't even allowed to *trick* a confession out of a lying son of a bitch. Lord knows how we'll ever put 'em away if that day ever comes. But why worry about it? Why not turn him over to Nebraska and let *them* hang him on material evidence?"

The Utah lawman started to ask a dumb question, brightened, and said, "By the Angel Moroni's halo!

Killing Professor Lewis so cruel in Omaha *was* premeditated, with no possible bull about machinery put out of order unintentionally!"

Longarm nodded soberly and said, "I'll get off a night letter to a pretty good district attorney I know in Omaha. They'd already got the forensic evidence on the professor's death, read wrong the first time. If you ship them that ballet dancer, with that nastier although correct drum in her base, that ought to convince judge and jury only a trade-school machinist could have set such a trap for a man he had a good motive to murder."

The Utah lawman grinned like a mean little kid and said, "You ain't bad at setting traps your ownself. You don't like crooks at all, do you?"

Longarm grimaced and replied, "Why did you think I chased them all over creation at a lousy six cents a mile, because I *loved* the sons of bitches?"

# Epilogue

A week and a half later, back in Denver, Longarm found himself in that same leather chair, searching in vain for an ashtray, while that banjo clock ticked on that oak-paneled wall and old Marshal Vail took way too long to read the final report Longarm had typed up for him over the weekend with the help of Miss Bubbles, down the hall in the stenography pool. They'd *had* an ashtray in that deserted office he and Miss Bubbles had wound up in after hours.

Billy Vail finally lowered the four typewritten pages to blow smoke back at Longarm and declare, "What I said about my roast-beef sandwiches still goes. But all right, this time you done us proud. The Uinta Agency reports them Indian Police got Kimoho Joe before a B.I.A. hearing alive and well, thanks to you. The breed and his woman would likely want to thank you too. They'd have hung Kimoho Joe for certain in Boulder County. The B.I.A. let him off on self-defense, and enrolled the two of them as paid-up reservation Utes."

Longarm shrugged, flicked ash on the rug to discourage any carpet mites, and said, "Beats working for a living, I reckon. I knew how you felt about needless expense to the federal government. So that was why I talked Utah and Nebraska, between them, to share costs on them surviving crooks. Harmon only named eight others, all of them small-time shits who were only following orders with no clear idea what was really going on."

Vail growled, "I can read. I'd never let my old woman read a lot of what's in *here,* though, and they're going to have to try Raymond Harmon in a closed court. You say Harmon's wife is pretty and that you had a time calming her down afterwards? Just how did you go about that, you charming rascal?"

Longarm laughed incredulously and replied, "Not that way, for Pete's sake. Aside from being sort of flat-chested, I suspect she was more than a mite displeased with me for exposing her man as a killer, even though he'd killed her father and was planning to kill *her.* That Colonel Palmer has offered to buy her out and let her sort of retire from the tent show business."

Vail nodded. "Then I take it this Rosemary O'Dowd you've cited for assisting must be built a little better?"

Longarm smiled sheepishly and confessed, "Like a brick shit-house, but alas, she left Ogden even before the others, to set things up for them in Virginia City. Didn't you read them pages in your very hand, Boss? They've promoted her from popcorn gal to their advance agent. I was the one who convinced her she could trust the sort of dumb but honest Colonel Palmer."

Vail said, "I read, I read, and there ain't one word in here to explain how come you wound up all your business with the local law in Ogden on a Friday afternoon, ten days ago."

Longarm said, "Hell, Billy, it was getting late, I'd just done what you just called a fine job, and don't you think

I deserved a Saturday night in a railroad center?"

Vail looked dubious and growled, "A railroad center run by the Church of Jesus Christ of the Latter-day Saints? But all right, far be it from me to suggest Cheyenne or Denver might be more fun for a growing boy. How come you didn't head back the next Monday, or even Wednesday, after seeing the last of all them tent-show gals, flat-chested or otherwise?"

Longarm blew an innocent smoke ring, and followed it with his gun-muzzle-gray eyes as he replied, convincingly enough, "Well, you see, I had these borrowed books to return to this patent lawyer's office, and his secretary told me he was out of town. So it seemed only right I hang around and make sure such valuable tomes didn't go astray."

Billy Vail resisted the temptation. He had little patience with dumb questions himself, and so he didn't have to ask how far astray Longarm might have led anything or anybody else.